I0665699

Sweet Justice:

A Mother's Revenge

Tameka Pleasants

PLEASANTS | PUBLISHING

VIRGINIA

For mothers who love unconditionally.

"Publishing media that inspires, educates and uplifts, one mind at a time."

Printed in the United States of America

First Printing, 2016

ISBN 13: 978-0692395226

Cover Art Designed by James Pressley

Please contact Pleasants Publishing for all media or order requests at:

pleasantspublishing@yahoo.com

Pleasants Publishing, LLC
Richmond, VA

www.pleasantspublishing.wordpress.com

www.amazon.com/author/tameka

www.facebook.com/pleasantspublishing

Acknowledgements

There is so much to acknowledge and be thankful for as I celebrate the publishing of this book, the accomplishment of another goal, and addition of another piece of my life's beautiful puzzle.

It's without question that I thank God first. None of this would be possible without Him. I know and truly believe that in my heart. I didn't choose writing, it chose me and I'm so grateful for this gift. It makes me feel good when the reader can connect with my words. God put writing in my soul and I look forward to writing and publishing many more works in the future that help me use this blessed gift from our Lord.

Each time I acknowledge my husband Fred in my books, I like to think that I give our love a little bit more immortality. Long after our bodies leave this earth people will know the love and adoration I felt for my husband and the family we created together. Millions of years from now people will still know that I found the best friend and partner in the man that I love and am creating a legacy with and I'm cool with that. I love you honey, thanks for being the best!

I used to group all of my kids together in one acknowledgement but I have to shout them all out individually because well, if you know them, you know why. They are all so different in personality and character yet they all look just alike.

They all need their individual moment in the spotlight because they are just that special.

I'll start with Fred 5 since I've known him the longest. There's a lot to be said about this guy. He's smart, well-read, handsome, caring and thoughtful; qualities that are hard to come across in pre-teens these days much less young men. He has a big heart for people, animals and a sincere passion to help. I know He has great things in store for him.

King is my middle son, my impassioned fighter. He feels very strongly and deeply about things. For a seven-year-old he has a great ability to comprehend and understand complex things or problems. King puts his all into everything he does and he takes learning and his education seriously. His competitive spirit drives him to consistently learn and master new things.

My youngest son with the out of this world personality is Cassius. Like his namesake Muhammad Ali, Cassius has the flare and extensive vocabulary of the Champ. Cassius is a loving boy with a huge imagination and desire to invent and create. You can always count on Cassius to say something that will either wow, shock/amaze you or make you laugh out loud.

The youngest and only girl in my bunch is Praise. Yes, Praise was named to give praise to God. She is a constant reminder of God's promises come true, all of my kids are but Praise the most. Most people didn't think we had a girl in us. Our family and friends had predicted a brood of all boys for us but God had something else in mind when He gave us our princess. Praise is very much a girly girl under the tough tutelage of her big brothers. She likes to look and feel pretty but she's no prissy chick. You won't leave her behind because you'll be too busy trying to catch up to her. Yet she is still the sweetest little girl that I've ever had the pleasure of knowing.

Next I want to thank and acknowledge my mother in law Carol Pleasants for her commitment and success in her recovery. Starting over is never easy at any age, when you're over a certain age it can look daunting and undoable. She is true example of courage and determination in the face of adversity. She remains a consistent source of love and support to our family.

The best thing about the present is the birth of tomorrow and the possibility that lies in the future. I have to thank my mom Valerie and my sister Ashley for being the true "fam" in family. It feels good to know that we have your love and support, and we hope you both know you have ours.

I can't forget to thank Mr. P, my father in law. Our corner has always been strong because of your presence and we appreciate all that you do.

There's a lot of other people I'd like to thank but I'd be running through pages and pages of paper and ink. If you consider yourself family or a friend of mine, thank you. Thanks for reading this book! Thanks for supporting my craft, my artistry...my love. I pray you enjoy it as much as I enjoyed writing this.

This book has been six years in the making, it's been changed many times and undergone many rewrites and revisions. It's been a source of great pride and fear. Yet it's here and I'm grateful.

Peace and Blessings,

Mek

CHAPTER I:

WHAT THE TWERK?

Tiffany took a long sigh as she pulled her too old rusted green 1996 Toyota Camry into her recently paved expensive driveway.

"Home finally," she breathed relieved. Even though it was only six o' clock in the evening it was already very dark out and looked to be about midnight. The street lights were on, and her freshly manicured lawn was illuminated beautifully by the overpriced solar lawn lights she had put down along her driveway and walkways two weeks ago.

Officer Tiffany Kimani Saunders had just finished her shift at the police department and was dying to get out of her uniform. For the past few weeks Tiffany had taken on extra hours and shifts to cushion her paychecks so she could get through the rough patches. She wasn't struggling but the expenses of raising a 16 year - old young lady seemed to increase by the thousand every day. That's for a regular child, if you had an ambitious one like Tiffany did, you had to keep them engaged in extracurricular activities and sports. The never ending fees, uniform costs, physicals, and fundraisers all wore on Tiffany's wallet but she felt good that she had the chance to make up for the short fall versus have Princess miss out on once in a lifetime - opportunities because she couldn't afford to pay.

"Oh well the solar lights do look nice. The ones in Dollar Tree are probably just as nice," laughed Tiffany to herself as she mocked her cheapness. She grabbed her duffel bag and purse off the backseat and headed inside. She never bothered to lock the car doors at night. Who was really going to steal her car? They would be doing her a huge favor.

The closer Tiffany got to her front door the louder the music coming from inside sounded. Immediately her instincts made her suspicious of what was going on inside her home. Certainly Princess had been guilty of listening to her music loudly but never as loud as it currently was being played. There was no need to put her key in the front door because it was already cracked open. Tiffany put her duffel bag and purse down on the porch and retrieved her weapon from its holster. She entered her house quiet and cautiously with her service weapon drawn, a .357 SIG. Tiffany checked all the rooms downstairs. The first floor was clear. She then headed straight towards her daughters' bedroom. The closer she got the clearer and louder the music got; it was her daughter's newest favorite song of the week, Beyonce's "7/11".

Tiffany couldn't hear anything above the music, so she swung the door open without knocking. On the other side of the door stood her daughter Princess and her best friend and neighbor Tyshelle dressed sexily in tank tops and booty shorts bent over twerking on camera. The new I Phone 6 that she had just purchased for her daughter was propped on the cell case stand recording the whole sordid show.

"Are you out of your damn mind," asked Tiffany as she put her weapon back into its holster.

Caught off guard and clearly busted Princess and Tyshelle panicked and start scrambling and grabbing their clothes off the floor to get properly dressed.

"Mom, I know it looks bad but we were just trying to see how we looked. We weren't going to upload it or anything I swear," pleaded Princess.

"And you think that makes it better Princess?" screamed Tiffany disgusted with her daughter.

"Auntie please don't be mad at us," begged Tyshelle.

"Girl why are you even worried about how I feel, you need to get home quick. I'm about to call your Daddy right now!"

"Oh my God, please don't call him," pleaded Tyshelle crying.

"I can't believe you're still talking to me. Girl bye!"

Tyshelle picked up her book bag and cell phone and made a break for the door.

Tiffany points at Princess, "you! Give me the phone now!"

"Mom I'm sorry," said Princess carefully handing over her phone while still trying to keep her distance.

"I can assure you it's taking everything in me to not knock your head clean off. Start cleaning up! I don't want to hear you breathe while I think about this dumb shit that you got going on now. And I got to call Ty's parents and let them know too," she said walking off in haste.

Tiffany remembered her bags on the porch and brought them in before getting her cordless kitchen phone from its charging base and dialing the number 2 speed dial to her neighbor's house next door. It rang and rang until TyRod Covington, the father of Tyshelle and the whole Covington clan answered the phone.

"Hello," answered TyRod out of breath.

"Hey man you alright?" asked Tiffany.

"Yeah I was outside balling with these youngsters. You know they say I'm getting old?" he asked not expecting an answer, albeit a truthful one.

"They tell the truth sometimes Rod."

"What? There you go. What you want anyway? My wife is still at work."

"I know that's why I called you. She doesn't need to deal with this shit on her job."

"What's going on?"

"I don't even know how to say this."

"What?"

"I just caught Princess and Tyshelle in her room recording a twerk video on their cellphones."

"What?"

"I said, I just caught Princess and Tyshelle in her bedroom recording a twerk video on her phone."

"I heard you the first time I'm just trying to process what you said. A twerk video?" he asked dumbfounded by what he was hearing.

"Yes, they had the music jumping, they got on the booty shorts and they J's giving it up on the camera."

"Oh my God. Is it online?" he panicked.

"They said they didn't upload it."

"Is it other videos?"

"I've been checking their pages regularly. I haven't seen anything but I haven't had a chance to go through Prin's phone just yet. I just wanted to let you know because I sent Ty home but I know she didn't come and volunteer that information."

"She sure did not. Home girl breezed in and went straight to her room talking about doing homework. I should have known something was wrong then. Thanks for the info. I'm about to go straighten her out right now."

"Tell Myshelle to call me when she gets settled in."

"Alright girl, will do. Goodnight."

"Night Rod."

Tiffany tried to mask her frustrations by breathing deeply and trying to think about exactly what she intended to do to her daughter. What punishment was appropriate for an inappropriate twerk video? She tried to think what would her mother do? She then realized if she did what her Mom would do, she would probably have to arrest herself. She could embarrass her daughter publicly. Tiffany had been seeing more viral videos on Facebook and YouTube of parents going through extremes to thwart bad behavior in their children. Tiffany called it digital discipline. She decided against that. Lord knows what her daughter was already doing for likes. Tiffany had seen a lot over the course of her life, especially since she had become a police officer. She was in no way shape or form prepared to deal with the issues that were beginning to arise with her teenage daughter Princess Sunshine Saunders, a rising senior at L.C. Bird High School.

Times like this Tiffany wished she had a husband, boyfriend, baby daddy, big brother, uncle, hell, somebody else that she could rely on to help her raise her daughter. Princess father William had been in and out of her life, never playing a consistent and stable position in their lives. Sitting on the bar stool with her face in her hands, Tiffany felt helpless as she closed her eyes contemplating her next move.

"Mom," whispered Princess.

"Yes Princess," said Tiffany unfazed, eyes still closed shut.

"I'm sorry. I know you're mad at me ... I'm sorry."

"Princess I appreciate your apology but I can assure you that is not going to help you avoid being punished."

"Can we talk about it?"

"What is there to talk about? I'm just stunned."

"Well do you want to know why we were recording the video?" Princess asked.

"Not really. What good reason could you possibly have for cutting up those perfectly good jeans to expose your little ashy butt cheeks to shake in front of the camera?"

"Ty and I want to enter the talent show at our Homecoming Rally."

"And you think that twerking on stage is a classy act?"

"No, it's not the classiest thing to do but we were practicing for the show."

"Well that certainly changes the way I feel about this situation. Maybe I should get in on the act too? I think I got some old booty shorts from back in the day that I can throw on to perform with you," Tiffany mused sarcastically.

"Huh?" asked Princess confused.

"Sounds stupid don't it?"

"But Ma," she whined.

"Princess please leave me alone before I lose this blessing of composure that has come over me."

Princess stormed off in a fit. Tiffany was close to yanking some sense into her but she had grown tired of the manner in which she was dealing with her daughter. Princess was getting older and whipping her butt was getting harder. Besides she wanted to impact her daughter in a way that caused her to think about what she was doing and change it. Physically punishing her child was a last resort. She wholeheartedly believed that violence created more violence. There had to be an alternative.

Clueless Tiffany retreated to her bedroom to undress and unwind after her long day. She changed into her favorite pajamas and cozy slippers before heading back downstairs to the kitchen to cook dinner. She looked at the pack of thawed chicken breasts in the refrigerator multiple times before deciding that cooking was out of the question. She slammed the refrigerator door shut. Since

Princess was now an unofficial member of the Twerk Team she could certainly fend for herself for a night. The carton of Banana Split ice cream called Tiffany silently from inside the freezer. She found the biggest spoon in the cabinet drawer she could and retired to her bedroom where she slammed her door behind her. Halfway through the carton Princess knocked on the door.

"What?" yelled Tiffany who didn't budge from her bed to open her door.

"What's for dinner?"

"Whatever you can twerk up!"

"Ma! You're not cooking?"

"No ma'am, eat some noodles or something."

"Noodles?"

"Princess if you don't back away from my door I am going to rip that mother off its hinges. Fix a sandwich. Its hot pockets in the freezer...hot wings. Figure it out. Bye."

Princess had some nerve but Tiffany could only blame herself. Surely she was proud of the young woman she was raising Princess to be. She was beautiful, smart, bright, energetic, and incredibly sweet; a scholar roll student, cheerleader and student council member. Yet the last six months had proved challenging for them both as Princess' body had transformed almost overnight.

It was like one night she went to sleep a sweet gangly little girl and the next day she woke up with more assets than she could handle at her age or any age for that matter. It was a huge adjustment because Princess liked the change in her body and had begun to dress too old for her age which in turn began to attract the wrong kind of attention from men and women alike. According to Princess the dikes were more aggressive than the boys she went to school with. What was Tiffany going to do?

By the time Tiffany felt her spoon scrape the bottom of the ice cream carton instantly she knew that dinner was over. As she walked back to the kitchen to dispose the empty carton in the trash she caught a glimpse of her daughter in the den eating and studying. She almost had to take a double take because for a second she saw her daughter as an adult, not the unprepared and uncertain version of herself that was preparing to take the PSAT's. On her way back to her bedroom she decided to check up on exactly what Princess was studying.

"What'chu studying?" asked Tiffany nosily.

"American History."

"Okay, you need any help?"

"No ma'am, I'm just finishing up this essay … but you can proofread it for me when I'm done. I know you're good at spotting stuff that's wrong. I guess that's the police officer in you," joked Princess.

"Ha ha ha very funny Miss Thing! I will certainly proofread your paper when you are done. Are your clothes ready for school on Monday?"

"Not yet, I'm undecided on what to wear."

"Why, what's going on?"

"Nothing really. There's this new guy in my class and he's cute and not a jerk."

"So you want to impress him?"

"No…not really. I just want him to notice me."

"And what do you think will get his attention?"

"Truthfully?"

"I almost don't know if I can handle the truth," sighed Tiffany.

"Ma, get your mind out the gutter! No, he's not that type of guy. Truthfully I think he'd notice me in something conservative yet cute. The girls in my class are throwing themselves at him, wearing short skirts, low cut cleavage, too high heels and he doesn't look like he cares."

"Well that's good, he's not …," Tiffany almost asked.

"No Mom he's not gay. He's just a cool guy. I don't know how to describe it. He's different, at least that's the way he comes off."

"My advice would be to be yourself. Honey you're a beautiful girl, you don't need to go so hard, attract him with your personality, your sense of humor or better yet your intelligence."

"So what would a beautiful girl with lots of personality, a great sense of humor and the brain of a genius wear?" asked Princess sincerely.

"Let's go see what's in your closet," said Tiffany signaling Princess to follow her upstairs. Once inside Princess' bedroom Tiffany went straight to the closet, filtered through a few items quickly and confidently pulled out the best look for her daughter.

"I really need a bigger closet Mom."

"Moving right along," said Tiffany ignoring the statement.

"Ma!"

"This," said Tiffany pulling pieces from her daughter's closet and draping them across her bed.

Surprisingly Princess liked the outfit that her Mom had picked out, a pair of blue jeans, a lacy cream tank top and a tiffany blue blazer with wheat penny loafers.

"That's cute but I got to hook it up with my accessories, you know put that little touch of glitz and glam on it," explained Princess.

"I know you will, pick out four more equally cute outfits and you're good for next week."

"Thanks Ma."

"Your welcome honey bunch. I'm going to bed now. We still need to talk about twerk fest in the morning."

"Ma don't call it twerk fest. It was practice."

"Twerk practice...fest. It's all the same thing."

"So now I'm talentless for the show."

"No you have way more talents than twerking. Figure it out."

"Yes sir," mocked Princess.

"Good night Princess, I love you anyway."

"Night Ma, I love you too."

Back inside the comforts of her bedroom Tiffany pushed the Pandora icon on her cellphone so the soft lulling music from her favorite "quiet storm" station could take her to Dreamland. She didn't even realize she had the silliest smile of satisfaction plastered on her face as she laid down to rest. Her only daughter was almost an adult, a spitting image of her at that. At almost six feet tall and her heaviest weight of around 185, Tiffany was still a brickhouse by any standard. Her limbs were long and lean like a dancer. She kept her hair dark black and shoulder length so it framed her doe like eyes and thick lips. It was hard enough being a woman and much harder raising one with all the same beauty attributes and more. It caused Tiffany much unrest on a regular basis yet she managed to forget her latest concerns and drift off to sleep.

Once she was in Dreamland the alarm clock was going off way too soon ending another mediocre night of sleep. She jumped up without hesitation because she hated the way the Snooze Alarm sounded; somehow it was slightly more annoying than the initial wake up alarm. Out of bed she kept her morning routine simple yet practical. After brushing her teeth, she got on her elliptical machine for 30 minutes before completing 30 pushups. Every morning she did this without fail and for Tiffany this was a good release of toxins and a great start to her day. Usually after her workout Princess would be stirring so Tiffany would start breakfast for them both while she got ready to go to her full time job as a Police Officer with the Richmond Police Department.

As Tiffany scrambled 2 eggs in a pan she remembered the few pieces of bacon she saved from a previous night's dinner and began cooking that in a separate pan. By the time Princess arose from her slumber the smell of bacon and eggs wafted through the house like Waffle House after the club on Saturday night.

"Hmm, it shole' smell good in here Ma," said Princess rubbing her stomach anxiously.

"Good Morning Princess. Flattery will get you everywhere," said Tiffany planting a quick kiss on her daughters' cheek.

"Oh I'm gone tear this food up. Thank you Mommy," gushed Princess while grabbing a ceramic plate from the cabinets and piling food on it.

"It's some croissants and banana nut muffins in the cabinet."

"This is perfect. I'm trying to cut back on the bread and stuff."

"Cut back?"

"Yes Ma. I need to keep my figure tight and right."

"You are 16, what problems could you possibly have with your figure?" laughed Tiffany.

"None and that's how I'd like to keep it."

"I hear you. I'm going to shower. I'm waiting on a phone call. Please answer the phone and bring it to me if it rings okay?"

"Yes ma'am. Who you waiting on?" Princess asked being nosey.

"Your father."

"What you call him for?"

"Grown folk business."

"To talk about me? Why did you call him? He doesn't care about me," Princess pouted.

"That's not true Princess. He does care...he's just trifling at times. And please don't go back and repeat that to him even if it is true."

"If he cared he would have shown up for my competition, I invited him weeks in advance. I sent him the reminder texts and even called his wife to ask if she would remind him. He doesn't care and I don't want you talking to him about me."

"Well the last time I checked I'm the parent and I know what's best. I understand your frustration with your father, believe me I do but ... he wants to be in your life. He wants a relationship with you. We just have to be patient with the process."

"And wait how long Ma? I'm 16 for Christ sake! You don't think it's funny that his interest in a relationship with all 11 of his kids came after he supposedly found God?" she said putting emphasis on the rabbit ears she held up while she spoke.

"See Princess that is the difference between you and me. I don't spend my time trying to figure out why Will does the things he does. I gave that up a long time ago. I just go with the flow and try to keep things as peaceful as possible so you can have everything you need and then some."

"I'm just saying Ma, please stop calling him about me. I'm begging you."

"No and you better answer that phone if he calls. If I get out of the shower and you allowed me to miss that call I'm going to whip your ass, straight up!"

"I got you Ma."

Tiffany walked off before she said something else. Princess loved to challenge her mother when she knew she probably shouldn't. Princess knew exactly what buttons to push and what buttons she should stay away from for fear of her life. Inside her shower stall Tiffany prayed to God for help as the hot water ran all over her body. Normally she would have put on a shower cap but this morning she didn't care as the water killed what little curl she had left in her hair. Six minutes into her shower the door opened and there was Princess's extended arm handing her the house phone.

"It's him," said Princess angrily.

"Thanks, let me get out of here," said Tiffany turning the shower off and grabbing her towel off the towel rod and wrapping herself in it while taking the phone.

Princess whispers, "I'll be locked in my room If you need me."

"Okay. Hello," said Tiffany into the phone receiver.

"Hey. How are you?" asked William Knoll, Princess's father.

"I'm good. How about you?"

"No complaints. God is still on the throne."

"Yes he is. Amen to that. How's Cindy?"

"She's good. I see Prin is still upset with me."

"Yeah she's still a little salty about you missing her cheer competition."

"I've got to make it up to her."

"Definitely but before you make it up to her, just make yourself more available to her. I know you've got 10 other children and 4 other mothers to deal with but Princess is the oldest and before you know it she'll be grown."

"I know I've been thinking about that a lot lately."

"I just need your help. Raising her at this age is getting hard. She's starting to smell herself and it's taking everything in me not to knock her out sometimes."

"Well definitely don't do that," said Will.

"What do you suggest I do? I walked in last night and her and Tyshelle was recording a twerk video to practice for their performance in the talent show."

"Twerk video. Oh Lord!"

"Yes, a twerk video, booty shorts and all. Cheeks hanging out, just stank."

"Where is she getting this from?"

"Not me. I'm not running around twerking or acting like that. It's everywhere, television, social media, school. It's everywhere."

"Did you try taking her phone," he asked.

"Of course I have. Her phone is not the problem, I've been working more hours lately and she's in here alone a lot. Maybe if we could arrange for her to spend time with you all or at the church helping out that would ensure she's not here alone doing stuff she has no business doing."

"That sounds like a good idea. Let me run it by Cindy first and then we will set something up."

There was a long awkward pause as Tiffany thought about her next choice of words. She had learned that she had to stay on target with Will so she just sat there with her phone in her hands as she reacted to what was just said to her.

"Tiffany? Hello … did she hang up?" asked Will.

"No I'm still here. I was just thinking."

"I see how you want to take that but Cindy is my wife, I have to check with her and make sure we can accommodate this arrangement or else she's just going to be sitting at my house unsupervised doing stupid stuff," he blurted.

"First of all I respect that Cindy is your wife, I respect that she is your partner and there are certain things you have to check with her about but your daughter is not one of them. Princess was your daughter well before Cindy ever became your wife, hell before you found God, so I don't think that there should be any speculation about whether or not she can come to your home or church in the evenings after school. Secondly you have 10 other children. Your house is never empty. I see this as a good opportunity to become a better father to your daughter."

"You are right about being a better father but I still have to clear it with Cindy first. I just need Cindy to not be surprised by all of this she's already dealing with a lot. Princess is welcome in our home anytime, just tell me what to do and I'll make sure she's taken care of while you work in the evenings. We would love to have her."

"Thank you. This is going to be good for you guys. I can see it now, father and daughter selfies at the church. Color coordinated outfits. This is going to be cute, I can't wait. She is going to love this...once she gets on board with it."

"Yeah that's the thing. Princess is just like you. She doesn't play and she don't hold back sometimes. I need her to be respectful of me and Cindy especially around the church. I know she bears a lot of resentment towards me but I want us to have a fresh start."

"How about you come by for dinner tomorrow evening? We'll sit her down and have a talk with her. Princess is a good kid, she is just very wounded by your absence and the fact that you had so many more children after her."

"I know it hurts. It hurts me that I ever did that to her but I've been avoiding dealing with this situation, kind of putting it off because of how she makes me feel about it. I see I just got to man up with this and make sure my baby gets all the right attention and love from her father, not one of these boys out here or even worse some grown man. I'll be there around 8."

"Wonderful. Tell Cindy I said hi."

"Certainly. Goodbye Tiffany. Tell Princess I love her."

"I will, bye."

Tiffany hung up the phone proud that the conversation with Will had gone well. She wasn't convinced he was one hundred percent in without Cindy's stamp of approval, so she just prayed for the best. She was mad that she had set herself up to cook dinner when she hated cooking. She wasn't bad at it; she just didn't have time for it. What would she cook?

CHAPTER II:

THE FIRST SUPPER

At 5am Tiffany was wide awake and unable to go back to sleep. It was Saturday, her off day so she wasn't rushing to get ready for work. A creature of habit she jumped right up and got her daily workout done before heading downstairs to the kitchen to fix her breakfast, a fruit and vegetable smoothie. Lucky for her Saturdays meant that Princess was on self-service for breakfast unlike the weekdays that Tiffany rose early to fix it for her. As Tiffany blended her smoothie she turned on the laptop that was always conveniently resting in the kitchen. Her 10-year service anniversary was fast approaching and she hadn't even thought about the party her friends were throwing her to celebrate the ten years she had served the Richmond community as a Police Officer. With nothing on her agenda Tiffany decided it was a good time to start looking for a dress. If her memory served her right she still had about a month before the party.

That was more than enough time to find the perfect dress and date for that matter. Who would she take with her? Tiffany wasn't dating anyone at that moment so she was clueless as to who would accompany her to her party. She had met a cute guy when she was on patrol last week but she tried to keep her personal and business affairs separate. He did give her his number. Maybe she would call him. Date or no date she was not going to be able to get out of the party. She tried to deter her friends from throwing it but they had convinced her that she had earned the right to celebrate.

If anyone knew of the changes Tiffany had made in her life ten years ago it was definitely her closest friends Myshelle, Dee, Ally and Jessie. Ten years ago Tiffany stunned her friends and family when she revealed she was accepted into the police academy and was pursuing a career in law enforcement. It was considered so left field for Tiffany who had never shown any interest in law enforcement before in her life. At that time, she was looking to be a part of something bigger that would allow her to provide a good safe life for her daughter. There were many friends and family who didn't understand why she would become a police officer and tried to call her a sell-out. Then there were the naysayers who doubted if she could complete police academy successfully. Tiffany proved those people wrong but more importantly she proved to herself that she was capable of achieving anything if she truly put her best effort into it. On the brink of such a momentous and celebratory occasion Tiffany was in deep reflection about where she started ten years ago and where she was at the present moment. Even though she was proud of her accomplishment she couldn't help but feel awkward about celebrating her career in law enforcement when there was so much negativity in the media involving police officers.

Every time you turned on your television there was a new report about a death of a civilian committed by an officer and the public's perception of law enforcement was changing every day. People were distrustful of police officers. This made it extremely hard to maneuver throughout the communities in a way that allowed Tiffany to help more people. Each day it felt like people were becoming more hostile and enraged. Truly Tiffany felt like she was fighting for her life every day, every encounter was beginning to feel like it could be her last. She owed it to her daughter to make the best decisions for them both and her career in law enforcement was feeling more like a death sentence every day. What would she do? What could she do?

Tiffany needed to be able to transition into another career, something less dangerous with more income. She needed to be flexible to accommodate Princess' ever changing schedule and schooling needs. It wasn't a lot of things she was good at so she began to feel hopeless. She didn't want to feel forced to continue working as a police officer especially if it wasn't worth the risks involved. So while Tiffany was supposed to be shopping for party dresses she found herself looking up school programs for her next career. Princess walked in on Tiffany drinking the last of her breakfast as she completed college entrance applications online.

"That looks intense," said Princess hugging her mother.

"It is," yawned Tiffany.

"Whatchu' doing?"

"Applications for college."

"What?"

"Yep."

"Why? You got fired?" Princess asked scared.

"No! That's messed up."

"No Mom, that's reality. Myshelle got fired yesterday. It's hard out here trying to make it."

"What?"

"Who told you that?"

"Come on ma, who else?"

"You're right – that was a stupid question. I wonder why she didn't call me."

"Because she's probably feeling crappy. Ty said her Mom and Dad got into an argument this morning."

"I had no clue. I'll be back," said Tiffany grabbing her blue sweater off the back of the bar stool and putting it on. She sprinted next door to the Covington residence to check on her bestie, Myshelle Covington. Tiffany pressed the doorbell, "It's Tiffany."

"It's open," screamed Myshelle from the inside.

Tiffany bolted inside the door escaping the cold frigid air that the thin sweater couldn't shield her from. "Where you at?" yelled Tiffany.

"Upstairs in the loft," replied Myshelle.

Tiffany knew her best friend's house as well as she knew her own. They had been neighbors for the last eight years but best friends since they were children. As usual Myshelle was in her loft office surrounded by letters, bills and more paperwork than she could handle.

"Hey honey, I just heard. I'm so sorry," said Tiffany hugging her best friend tightly.

"Thanks babe. I'm doing okay," said Myshelle trying to be strong.

"Why didn't you call me?"

"I was still trying to process what happened and in my feelings."

"I can imagine. Rod tripping?"

"Of course he is."

"Where is he?"

"Gone to play basketball with his brother."

"Where the kids?"

"Ty had to work today at the boutique. Jr. is at practice and Michelle is with Joe and his family this weekend."

"You want to get out and do something today?"

"I wouldn't dare. Chile Rod might have a hernia if he thought I was spending some money without knowing when my next check is going to show up."

"I didn't say anything to you about spending any money, I asked if you wanted to get out and do something."

"I heard you but unless you picked up an African sugar daddy that I don't know about... I know you're strapped for money too. I don't need you digging yourself into no hole to make me feel better."

"See that's why you get on my nerves sometimes. I'll be back in an hour and a half to pick you up. Be ready."

"Where we going?"

"It's a surprise. Don't have me outside waiting forever on you either. I will bust up in this joint and put my handcuffs on you and drag you out."

"Well damn. You know I'm slow and I hate being restrained. You got to give me more time."

"Two hours' tops."

"Bet."

"Love you chick," said Tiffany leaving as fast as she arrived.

"Love you too," gushed Myshelle sentimentally.

Tiffany went back home to get ready for her outing with her best friend who was in need of a mental break from it all. Back at home Tiffany remembered her planned dinner with Princess's father. She texted herself a grocery list and found something in her closet to wear out. With time to spare Tiffany pulled out the curlers from her hair and finger combed her hair loosely causing the ringlets to frame her face beautifully. Tiffany smiled at herself in the mirror and found her favorite lip stain and applied a thick coat on her lips. Beautiful she thought. Now she was ready to go. She grabbed her cell phone from its charger and her purse from her closet. She peaked in Princess bedroom on her way to the door, "I'm leaving for a little while, going to take Myshelle out."

"Aww that's sweet of you Ma."

"Thanks, don't forget we have to talk tonight. So don't make any plans or leave before I get back home."

"Yes ma'am, I'm staying planted in this house."

"Good, call me if you need me. Love you."

"Love you too. Tell Auntie I'm sorry about her job but she always tells us when one door closes, another one opens."

"I will. Bye boo."

"Bye Ma."

When Tiffany walked outside Myshelle was sitting comfortably in the passenger side of her own vehicle, her beautiful red Range Rover. "Oh so you gone be on time and insult my car at the same damn time huh," laughed Tiffany.

"No I wouldn't dare insult you. I just figured we could take my car."

"Yeah yeah, lucky for you I like driving your car. Thanks it's like driving a free rental."

"See I knew it would make us both happy."

"You know me too well. Thank you my sister. My car blows in a major way but I can't afford to do anything about it at the moment," said Tiffany climbing in the SUV and adjusting the seat to her comfort.

"You know you can use my car anytime. It's not like I have anywhere to go anymore anyway."

"For how long though? You'll be working again before you know it."

"I hope so. That's 2 layoffs and now this in a five-year time period. That's a lot."

"I know."

"It's like every time Rod and I get back to some regular stuff, boom; another bomb just blowing the spot all up. It's getting harder and harder to juggle everything that's going on. His business is doing well but we just paid some bills off and were thinking of taking a vacation this summer... just the two of us."

"Let's not even focus on all that today. My goal is to get your mind off of everything if only for a few hours. So let's make a deal, we don't talk about jobs, men, kids or unhappy stuff for that matter," suggested Tiffany.

"That doesn't leave us a lot to talk about. That's my life in a nutshell right there."

"Stop playing there's lots of stuff to talk about. Let's just cut the radio on and have girl time like we used to do. You remember girl time?" asked Tiffany.

"I remember girl time. Girl time was the shit. We definitely need girl time."

"Let's do it. We need this. Girl time it is."

Tiffany and Myshelle started screaming together like pubescent teenage girls with out of control hormones, "Girl Time!"

Twenty something years of friendship and sisterhood had forged a bond between Tiffany and Myshelle that had survived some of life's greatest challenges and obstacles for the women. They were more like sisters than friends; being next door neighbors for almost the last ten years only made them closer and cemented the solid friendship that was already in place. It didn't hurt that they favored each other physically too. Now with both of their families in place they were all bona fide family and there was nothing that could be done to change that. Even though the Saunders family was considerably smaller than the Covington's they were all very tight and close knit. Over the course of their twenty-year friendship the young families had lived together, vacationed together, celebrated birthdays with combined parties, sleepovers and cookouts. They were so close that their 16-year-old daughters had become best friends and sisters of sorts too when they were toddlers.

The women's lives were deeply enriched by the other's presence. They were the kind of forever friends that most people dreamed about. Even now when Tiffany was uncertain as to what her financial future looked like with her concerns about her career in law enforcement she was still willing to go the extra mile to see a smile on her friend's face. Tiffany knew you couldn't put a price on "girl time" the name they came up for those rare moments when they could get out. "Girl time" was about having fun, being sassy, flirty and slightly kooky. Tiffany and Myshelle always had the best times and craziest experiences during their "girl time".

With their time all laid out Tiffany drove them straight to the Rose Spa, a place she had heard by recommendation from the wife of a fellow officer. They were being pampered with a deluxe spa package that included massages, manicures and pedicures. After they were primped and preened they felt relaxed and just giddy enough from the champagne to want more drinks and the adventure that followed. With a fresh coat of paint on their nails, a glow behind their smiles and the tension of life pooling at their feet, they decided to head to Kickback Jack's for drinks.

"That massage was everything girl. I really needed that. Thank you so much," said Myshelle applying a fresh coat of lipstick to her lips.

"You are so welcome. I'm glad you feel better. You look like you feel better."

"I do. That massage got all the kinks and knots out...almost all the kinks," she laughed.

"Lord, tame yourself girl. You know how that liquor makes you filthy," laughed Tiffany.

"I know. Loose in the caboose."

"You ain't never lied. You promise to behave?"

"I'm certainly going to try."

"Lord Jesus, please help us," prayed Tiffany as she gripped the steering wheel tightly.

Inside the bar Tiffany and Myshelle found an empty table that they claimed for their own. It was in a good spot where they could see everything and it was in close proximity to the bar. The waitress took their initial order and opened a tab on Tiffany's credit card. Myshelle started off with a heavy hitter, a double of Patron with a Vodka and cranberry to chase it. Tiffany was way subtler with a glass of white wine. Myshelle practically inhaled her shot and was already half finished her other drink as Tiffany sipped her wine slowly scanning the room while trying to enjoy herself. She loved to drink socially but sometimes hated the bar scene especially being a police officer. A lot of times she found herself policing the joint instead of having a good time. The further away she got from law enforcement in her mind the easier it was for her to let her guard down. Soon Tiffany's wine glass was empty and she second guessed whether she should have another drink. She wanted to be clear enough to drive home because she knew Myshelle was going to get wasted.

"I'm done," said Tiffany in defeat.

"What? Stop playing Tiff. You brought me out to have 1 drink."

"You've had 2 and can continue to drink if you like. I'm going to ensure we make it home safely."

"Don't be that girl tonight Tiff. Loosen up, have fun. Call one of them police officer friends of yours to pick us up if we get too turnt."

"Oh I bet they will call the police to come pick our black asses up," laughed Tiffany.

"It's girl time! Remember!"

"Yeah but..."

"No but's unless it's that fine man's butt in your hands or mine for that matter," screeched Myshelle.

"What? He is fine."

"I know. Let's get his attention."

"No," blurted Tiffany.

It was too late. Myshelle had already gestured for the man to join them at their table and he was eagerly headed straight towards them holding his drink in tow.

"How you ladies doing tonight?" he asked gingerly.

"Good, have a seat. I'm Mya and this is my best friend Tiffany. You are?" she asked extending her hand to shake his.

"I'm Nick, nice to meet you ladies. Thanks for inviting me over."

"So you single Nick?" asked Myshelle curiously.

"I am tonight."

"I can handle that," flirted Myshelle.

"I'm waiting on some friends of mine to show up. You mind if they join us?" Nick asked.

"Are they as fine as you are?"

"That's a crazy question. You asking me if my boys are attractive as I am? Let me think about that," he laughed.

"You know what she means Nick, don't be coy. Are your friends ugly or nice looking like you?" reinforced Tiffany.

"Whoa I thought you were the shy one? Guess I was wrong. You're the most forward one," he laughed harder.

"No you're wrong again Nick, she's the police officer one. Don't make her arrest you," flirted Myshelle.

"Word, you're an officer?" he asked intrigued.

"Yes sir."

"Damn, I've never seen a police officer as pretty as you."

"And you never will again," Tiffany advised.

"I can believe that. What are you ladies getting into tonight?"

"Nothing too serious," she replied.

"I feel that. Can I buy you ladies a drink?"

"Certainly, I'll take a shot of patron and my girl Tiffany will take something strong and stiff."

"Well well well, I don't even know how to respond to that. I'm blushing. That's a first," he laughed.

"What are you drinking?" asked Tiffany.

"Vodka tonic."

"I'll take one of those, sounds good."

Nick signaled the waitress for the drinks and pulled his cell phone out of his pocket and placed it on the table.

"Nice phone, do you mind if I look through it? It's a bad habit of mine," joked Myshelle.

"Sure I've got nothing to hide," he said sliding his phone across the table to her.

"So you mean to tell me you don't have any crazy phone lock; dick picks...nothing you trying to hide in your phone?"

Nick bowls over laughing, "What? Dick pics? Nah I can't say I do but if you want to see mine you should just ask. I'll show it to you."

"Good to know," said Myshelle putting his phone down.

"Lost interest?" he asked.

"In the phone, not you," she came back.

"That's good to know."

"When are your friends getting here?"

"Soon. Why?"

"I like being in the company of handsome men."

"Let me see where they at. They missing all the fun," he said texting his friends. As he sat his phone down on the table it started to buzz and vibrate.

The waitress showed up with their drinks just as Nick responded to his text message.

"I'm going to the bathroom. Behave," ordered Tiffany.

"I will," replied Myshelle.

Tiffany was tickled by Myshelle's brazen and aggressive tactics with men. She had been that way as long as she could remember. Hell that was how she got her husband whom she was conveniently forgetting about. Tiffany definitely didn't want Myshelle to do anything that would jeopardize her marriage but she had come to learn that she couldn't stop people from doing what they were going to do anyway. She would try to keep a leash on her friend for the evening but she knew Myshelle was a grown woman who did not like being controlled.

When Tiffany got back to her table from the bathroom Nick's friends had arrived and were standing around their table. Seeing Myshelle surrounded by a group of attractive men was all too familiar from their teenage days.

"Tiffany, Nick's friends and his baby brother are joining us this evening. Guys this is my bestie Tiffany."

"Nice to meet you gentlemen."

"I heard you're a fellow officer," said Nick's baby brother Nigel while pulling out her chair.

"Thank you, an officer and a gentleman," she remarked.

"Always. You in Richmond?"

"Yeah. You?"

"Chesterfield. I'm Nigel. This is my buddy Warren and our cousin Alex."

"Okay. Nice to meet you guys."

The group had drinks, laughed, joked, flirted and everything in between for the next three hours. Myshelle and Tiffany both were having fun when they realized that real life called them. Tiffany looked down at her watch and gasped in horror. It was after seven o' clock and she was supposed to be expecting Will for dinner at eight o' clock.

"Shit, we've got to go. I forgot I have dinner plans," exclaimed Tiffany.

"You're leaving?" asked Nigel.

"Yeah I've got to go."

"Date?"

"No, nothing like that. My daughter and I have to meet with her father for dinner. Parental issues."

"Okay I understand. Can I get your number?" Nigel asked playfully.

"I'm an officer; you know the answer to that. You can give me yours though," she said unlocking her cell phone to let him key in his number.

"I'd like to take you out one day," he said matter of factly.

"How old are you anyway?"

"30."

"You look younger."

"I'll take that as a compliment."

"We'll see. I'll call you."

"I'm delighted."

Tiffany smiled as she signaled Myshelle to get up. She was engrossed in her own conversation with Nick.

"We have to go now?" whined Myshelle tipsy.

"Yes, remember our families at home waiting for us?"

"Nick will take me home, right?"

"Like hell he will. I don't need any crimes being committed outside my house. Nick say goodbye to Myshelle, hope you two had fun but I'm returning her to her husband."

"He doesn't deserve her," Nick joked.

"Come on girl, let's go," said Tiffany urging her friend to leave.

"He doesn't deserve me," slurred Myshelle.

"We going to do this again soon?" Nick asked Myshelle.

"Maybe, I have your number. I can't make any promises though. I'm a Real Housewife," she joked.

"I'm a real gentleman. Be good girl," Nick said kissing Myshelle on the cheek.

"Always baby."

Once Myshelle was seated safely in the passenger seat of her truck Tiffany parted ways with Nigel, leaving him to dream about the hug and quick kiss she had planted on his cheek. Girl time had been successful because Myshelle was certainly not thinking about being jobless or angry with her husband. With no time to spare Tiffany sped thru Arby's drive thru and picked up a rotisserie family meal. It was not the homemade lasagna she had wanted to cook but it would have to suffice. After rushing through the traffic Tiffany pulled into her driveway behind Will's blue Dodge RAM truck. He was already inside. That had to be a good sign. At least Princess didn't have him waiting

outside till she got home. Tiffany escorted Myshelle into her own house, ran

back to the truck to retrieve dinner and her purse and was rushing hurriedly

through the door. When she walked into her house Will was sitting on the couch

flipping through the channels on the flat screen television and Princess was

nowhere to be found.

"Sorry I'm late. Where's Princess?"

"In her room," replied Will irritated.

"She's still acting stank."

"A little bit. What happened to you cooking dinner for us?" he said

eyeing the Arby's bag in her hand.

"Change of plans, I thought I would have time to cook but that ran dry

so I picked up Arby's. You cool with that?"

"Absolutely. Can I help with something?"

"That's sweet but I got this. Relax... can I get you something to drink?"

"Water please."

"Sure," she said putting her hostess hat on and retrieving a glass from

the cabinet that she filled with purified water from the faucet. She topped it off

with ice from the icemaker on the refrigerator door.

"Where are you coming from?" Will asked curiously.

"Kickback Jacks with Myshelle."

"Sounds like fun times."

"Yeah it was something like that."

"Are you dating anyone?" he inquired while trying to make small talk.

"Not really. How's Cindy?" asked Tiffany keeping busy with the food.

"Cindy's good. She said to tell you she said hello."

"Aww so sweet of her," gushed Tiffany sarcastically.

"It's hard to believe you aren't dating anybody. Why not? Princess is definitely old enough now and it's not like I'm not around."

"Why do you care?" Tiffany asked perplexed as she reached for the plates in the cabinet.

"Why wouldn't I care? You just seem a little lonely."

"Even if that were true I think we need to keep us out of these scenarios. After all these years we're finally in a good place. Let's keep it like that."

"My apologies, I wasn't trying to cross the line and I certainly wasn't trying to come on to you. I'm very much happy in my marriage and I would like the same for you, you deserve it. Even though we were never together I did see something special in you. I still see that in you. So again my bad, I'll stay on track."

Tiffany immediately felt bad. "I wasn't trying to say it like that."

"No you were completely right. I'm here to talk about our daughter."

"Yes! I'll go grab her," said Tiffany wiping her hands on the dish towel that hung from her double oven door handle. She then ran off to get Princess from her bedroom while Will waited on the couch. "Princess let's go. Your dad and I want to talk to you," yelled Tiffany as she approached her daughter's bedroom door.

"I'm sleep," replied Princess sarcastically.

"Real funny smart girl. Come down now, you have sixty seconds only," ordered Tiffany.

Tiffany headed back downstairs, she didn't want to leave Will unattended for too long, who knew what else he would want to talk about. As Tiffany's foot hit the bottom step Princess's bedroom door flung open. Princess was on her way downstairs to join her parents for a dreaded evening of conversation and dinner.

"Thank you for joining us Princess," said Tiffany.

"Your welcome mother."

"Good evening again Sweetheart," said Will jumping to his feet to embrace his daughter who was growing up more every day.

"Father," said Princess hugging him back.

"Don't be smug Princess," Tiffany snapped.

"I wasn't."

"It's okay Tiffany. Let's just have a good dinner. I'm glad your Mom invited me over. It seems like it's been forever since the three of us have had dinner together," said Will.

"I know. We need to do more family dinners," suggested Tiffany.

"Maybe we can get Cindy to arrange something at the house sometimes. We'd like to have you both join us at home sometimes."

"That sounds good."

"You know me and your mother are going to do whatever it takes to help you through whatever it is you're going through?" offered Will to Princess.

"What exactly do you think I'm going through?" Princess asked because she was dumbfounded as to why they were all in the same room together for dinner.

"Something, a phase...stage, I pray. You recording twerk videos?"

"Yes but why y'all acting like I made a porno?"

"You might as well have. You had your buttocks on display for the whole world to see," shouted Will.

"It's not appropriate Princess. Teenage girls should not be recording twerk videos and then uploading them for likes. You're better than that. Is that all you're good for? Shaking your butt so some boy can be impressed with you?" asked Tiffany.

"It's not about the boys Ma. I just like how I look when I dance."

"No that's not true because I didn't catch you dancing, I caught you twerking."

"It's just fun. Nothing serious, I'm not letting boys feel or touch on me. I'm not twerking on nobody and it's actually a good workout. Ma, you're all about your fitness you should give it a try."

"Princess!" shouted Will.

"What? She probably already twerking, I get my sick body from her and she just as vain as I am. That's where I get it from. This is totally not my fault."

Tiffany was utterly shocked at the words that had just flew out of her daughter's mouth and for a moment time stood still while she contemplated what to do. Without even thinking Tiffany had open handed slapped Princess across her face in disgust. "How dare you talk to or about me like that?" exclaimed Tiffany.

"You hit me?" cried Princess.

"You lucky I didn't knock your ass into next week. Are you kidding me Princess? A sick body! Where are you getting this crap from? I'll be damned if you pin this on me like it's my fault you turning into a thot."

"Whoa ladies," intervened Will jumping in between the mother and daughter.

"She hit me!"

"What are you telling him for? He should smack your ass too!"

"I'm not going to smack anybody. There's already been enough of that going on today. What I am going to do is ask you to pack yourself an overnight bag and come stay with me for the night? Your mother could use a break tonight but before you pack anything, you owe her an apology."

"Why do I have to leave?"

"Princess I didn't ask you to stay with me. I asked you to pack a bag and then apologize to your mother. Clearly it's some things we need to address but I don't see much more getting resolved tonight like this. Tiffany, you cool if I take her with me?" asked Will.

"Go right ahead," Tiffany gave in and threw her hands up.

"I'm going to the restroom. You two talk please," he pleaded.

"Okay I was wrong for what I said but you know what I meant. I was only trying to say that you're beautiful with a banging body and I was blessed with those same attributes. I shouldn't have been recording the twerk video," blabbed Princess.

"It didn't come out like that. What you said sounded like a stripper ready to take the pole...you are 16 Princess! What type of mother would I be if I let you do everything you wanted to? I've always tried to be the best example of what a lady is for you and it's very hurtful to see you doing these grown things. Not to mention it bugs me because you are a smart girl. You know that all attention is not positive attention and my concern is that the attention you're going to draw to yourself twerking on stage is going to diminish all the hard work that you've done studying and making good grades...you know being a scholar," explained Tiffany patiently.

"You're right Ma. I do know better. I'm sorry if I disappointed you and I will see if I can come up with another dance routine for my talent show that's more appropriate for my age. I never meant to let you down."

"You never have and you never will but I still have to try to steer you away from certain situations."

"You accept my apology Ma?"

"Of course I do sugar, give me a hug," said Tiffany extending her opened arms to her daughter.

Princess ran into her mother arms like she had so many times before and just got lost in her mother's love as she hugged her back tightly.

"I love you Mom."

"I love you too Princess. Can you do me a favor though baby girl?"

"Yes ma'am," agreed Princess.

"I need you to give your father a second chance. He's clearly here to help us both and I want to involve him more in your life. Use this opportunity to talk to him so you guys can move forward in your relationship. Don't be so hard on him. Forgive him. It's time," Tiffany urged.

"Okay. I'll do better," Princess agreed.

"I know you will. Now go pack your bag because I need a break from you girl! You almost got yourself shot tonight," laughed Tiffany.

"Oh my God you were gone shoot me Ma?"

"Maybe; it depended on what came out of your mouth next."

"I thought we was better than that."

"I still love you though. Now go get your stuff!"

Princess obeyed her mother and went to her bedroom to pack an overnight bag to take with her to her father's house. This would be the first time Princess stayed with her father and his new wife, it had been many years ago when she had last stayed with him. Tiffany was pleased that Will was able to intervene in the argument and keep it from escalating. She also appreciated the break from Princess. Lord knows she loved her daughter but it was constant work caring, loving and looking out for her. She was more than ready to share some of that burden with Will who was now wanting more responsibility and role in his daughter's life.

Surveying the kitchen Tiffany noticed the food was untouched; they had never even got a chance to eat because the tension went from 0 to 100. When Will came back downstairs Tiffany smiled at him earnestly.

"Is that a smile Tiffany?" he asked.

"It is."

"That's beautiful."

"Thanks...for everything. Your presence here made tonight a success."

"Thanks for having me. I want to help and I can help. I'm glad y'all fixed it, I hate seeing women upset with each other especially you two."

"Well how about we haven't even touched dinner? I invited you here to eat and you guys are getting ready to go."

"I wanted to keep it from getting explosive. Let's enjoy this dinner together first and then we'll head on our way."

"I like that. I'll make the plates," said Tiffany arranging food on three plates.

"I'm ready to go," said Princess carrying her bag on her shoulder.

"Let's eat first."

"Cool, I'm hungry anyway. And Ma knows I love those muffins from Arby's. They are so delicious!"

"They are good!" agreed Tiffany.

"What muffins?"

"Taste it," said Tiffany holding up a muffin.

Will took a bite and nodded in agreement, "that is good. Give me that muffin!"

They all laughed. It was the first of what they hoped would be many laughs together. Dinner was a success and it wasn't because the menu came out the way Tiffany planned. It wasn't unsuccessful because Tiffany ended up rushing home late or almost got into a fight with her daughter. It just all fell into place.

CHAPTER III:

PRINCESS AWAY, TIME TO PLAY

With Princess gone for the night with Will Tiffany was anxious to take advantage of her childless evening. Lord knows even at Princess age those moments were far and few. Tiffany rang Myshelle's cell phone but she didn't answer. That could only mean 1 of 2 things. She was either knocked out asleep or fussing with TyRod. And she very well may have fallen asleep after fussing with TyRod. Tiffany thought about her Number 4 speed dial but she decided against it. She needed something and she had an idea what it was but it was always ugly confronting the truth. Tiffany had a friend that she had known for many years that she allowed to "service" her. Maybe she should call Nigel. She definitely shied away from that idea... she had just met him. Tiffany was horny but not desperate. Lord knows Will was looking better in his older age if he wasn't married she certainly would have let him slice her pie. Most times she did a good job controlling her hormones but she couldn't deny that she still had needs and spots that needed to be touched by more than air and sunlight. Unbridled and controlled by the feelings that tingled from her stomach to her inner thighs she pressed the 4 on her screen and then the speakerphone button. Tiffany's stomach tightened in knots as the phone rang and rang. She hoped he wouldn't answer. He always did though. He looked forward to her calls as much as she looked forward to him answering.

"Hello," he bellowed into the phone.

"You sound like hot chocolate over the phone," Tiffany flirted.

"Oh but wait till you feel what I am in person," he shot back.

"You're doing well?" she asked.

"I'm alright. It's been a while since I've talked to you. I almost thought you forgot about me."

"I can never forget about you. I've just been super busy. Princess is...hell, I don't want to talk about her. It's been hectic. I wanted to call."

"Who me?" he joked.

"Yes you. What's funny about that?"

"You don't need me for much, well except for you know. I'm good for that shit."

"Damn you getting me wet right now. You sound so good," breathed Tiffany heavily.

"I do. You sound good too. You coming to see me?"

"Where you at?"

"I'm at the studio."

"I'll be there in a half hour."

"Word. I'll be waiting, you know I don't like to wait too long."

"I know. Bye," she hung up abruptly. She didn't like to be kept waiting either. Tiffany jumped into the shower and bathed quickly. She was out and completely moisturized from head to toe in seven minutes. She was dressing into her workout clothes and putting on her tennis shoes and then out of the door in 23 minutes flat. Tiffany jumped in her car and drove straight to the private studio Chris trained his clients in. Chris was another childhood friend who happened to be a personal trainer. She pulled into an empty parking space behind the studio he leased for his business. She dialed the numbers on the access keypad and was inside the studio before she knew it.

Tiffany located Chris in the main studio that was completely surrounded by mirrors. He wanted his clients to be able to see every angle, every muscle and movement. He was sitting on the floor stretching his long muscular legs out.

"Well well if it isn't my favorite non client and former best friend Tiffany Saunders."

"We on a two name basis now?"

"You tell me? I don't hear from you for months at a time except when you want me to work those kinks out your vagina muscles," he laughed.

"But you know why?"

"No I don't know why. Indulge me," he continued stretching.

"I was falling for you Chris. We're friends."

"So I can fuck you but I can't love you?"

"Your lifestyle is too much for me!"

"My lifestyle. I'm a physical trainer."

"I know and that's the problem. Thank God I'm not a client but I know you're fucking several of them. I hear about you."

"I'm a man, a single man at that. I like the company of beautiful women. Guilty as charged Officer Saunders."

"Don't call me Officer."

"But you are one. I should have told you to wear that uniform of yours so I can take it off of you."

"Boy please. If you so righteous why you answer my calls?"

"Because we're friends first. I miss you. I love you...I love having sex with you. Making love to you, whatever you want to call it. So I rather get your time when I can, then not at all. Come here," he motioned for her to sit with him.

Tiffany settled on the floor in front of him and put the bottom of her shoes against his. He reached for her hands and began to stretch her out gently and smoothly.

"I'm too insecure to be comfortable with the women you train."

"That's unfortunate. I'm a good guy. One of these days you're going to call me to scratch that itch of yours and I'm going to have to turn you down because I'm in a relationship; not because I don't want you."

"Today you're still single though."

"True. Come over here," he said pulling Tiffany's feet until she had slid across the floor and her legs were straddled around his waist. He pulled Tiffany in close and held her for a minute. His hands began to explore underneath her shirt and caressed her back down to her pants. He pushed through the waist line till he had her buttocks cradled in the palm of his hands like a basketball. He squeezed and rubbed her cheeks as she purred liked a kitten being rubbed by its owner. Chris had never been an ass man until he met Tiffany as a young boy. She was more developed than any of the girls in their grade or school. Tiffany stuck out like a sore thumb of sorts attracting stares, gazes, catcalls and lust. Chris had watched her grow from being shy about her assets to being a grown woman in control of her body and how it could pleasure them both. The fact was he still answered her calls because she drove him wild. The mere scent of her awakened an animal attraction in him that sent him over the edge every time.

"I'm sorry I've been anti. I know how that makes you feel. I never want you to think that our years of friendship amounted to a booty call. You're more than that to me. I just don't know how to deal with my feelings about you right now."

"I can understand that. Damn, you feel so good," he moaned.

"Like I said earlier I've been meaning to call you."

"Yeah, I remember."

"You know my ten-year anniversary on the police force is coming up and the girls are throwing me this big party. I would love it if you would accompany me and be my date for my party," said Tiffany looking into his eyes.

"Just say when and where. I'll be there."

"You will?"

"Of course, I didn't realize it had been that long. I'm proud of you. Everybody doubted whether you could complete the academy and look at you. That's good shit," he said embracing her tighter.

"Thank you. Ahh, that's such a relief. I didn't want to go by myself."

"Stop playing me T. I know its guys lined up to take you out."

"No, it's definitely not like that."

"Good, I'd like to keep it like that then," he joked.

"That's not right," whined Tiffany playfully.

"Why not? I'm keeping you all to myself."

"What you gone do when you have me all to yourself?" she teased.

"This," he said picking her up off the floor and carrying her to a weight bench in the corner. He placed her gently on the bench and then rolled her panties and pants off down her legs. He tossed them in the corner and kneeled down to wrap her legs around his head. His long wet tongue found her button and beyond. Her wetness welcomed his oral exploration. She rocked back and forth as he maneuvered his mouth all over her body. Her body craved his touch, she couldn't control the desire to pull his pants down and straddle him on the bench. She held on to his shoulders as she rode him unleashing all of her inhibitions, frustrations, desires and passions onto him. He was engrossed in her performance in the mirror and smacked her ass in satisfaction. She rode him harder. Her breasts smacked against his face as she climaxed on him. She didn't stop riding till she saw that familiar guttural facial expression and felt his grip release on her butt. She collapsed on the floor of the studio next to Chris who even in impeccable shape was worn from their lovemaking.

"So you would really cut lose all your other bunnies to lock into this...me...us?" asked Tiffany massaging his manhood sweetly.

"What?"

"You said you wanted me all to yourself?"

"Yeah tonight and any other night we kick it."

"I took that so wrong. What the hell is wrong with me? Am I that desperate?" exclaimed Tiffany in horror.

"Tiffany you know it's not like that."

"I know. I just don't know how to feel about this us situation. Don't get me wrong...the things that we do together keep me sane and levelheaded. I just feel like I'm wanting more than just the sex. Why can't the sex be the icing on the cake?"

"Because I'm not the only dessert in your bakery."

"What?"

"Don't play innocent Tiffany. You act like I won't lock into you but you won't lock into me! You've been playing around with the thought of giving me your heart but there's something holding you back. Maybe you know too much about me, my past, shit my present. I'm not chasing you because I don't want you. I see so much in you. You're a great mother, friend. You're good at your job. You're beautiful, who wouldn't want you? I'm no fool Tiffany but at the same time...I'm no fool Tiffany!" laughed Chris.

"I hear you. You right. I just get caught up because its times where I wish things were different. I guess I'm getting old Chris."

"You ain't getting old. You're getting better and sexier!"

"You're too sweet. I'm going to snatch you up one of these days. I'd be a fool to let you get away," Tiffany poured out.

"Till that day comes you can keep using my body for your own selfish reasons," he laughed.

"Perfect. I can handle those arrangements. Are you ready to fulfill more of your obligatory expectations?"

"I'm always ready," said Chris mounting Tiffany on the floor.

The following morning Tiffany woke up in the comforts of her own bed. It was nothing better than waking up in her comfy cushy bed after great sex. One of these days her man would be waking up next to her. Maybe that would be Chris. Maybe not. As hot and cold as her emotions ran she wasn't ready to stop seeing Chris altogether. She could still feel him pulsating through her body. She shivered in delight and retreated to stay in bed as long as she could. She rolled over to locate her phone that had gotten lost in her covers. The text on the screen from Will reassured Tiffany that things were going well with Princess.

Will: Tiff, hope I didn't wake you. Just wanted to let you know that Princess is having a good time here with her brothers and sisters. We figured you could use a longer break so I've picked up her some things from the mall to set her room up at the house. She's going to be with us another night or two as long as it's okay with you. Feel free to stop by anytime to check on her. Thanks for everything, we're having a great time together. See you soon.

That was good news to Tiffany's ears. As she closed her eyes to drift off to dreamland her phone rang out jarring her out of her lustful daydream. She didn't recognize the number but she didn't recognize half the numbers in her call log.

"Saunders."

"Officer Saunders we finally have the chance to speak again," said the man's voice.

"Who is this?"

"Guess?"

"I don't like to play guessing games."

"Nigel. Your pal from the bar the other day."

"Hey Nigel. You sound different over the phone."

"Really. People say that all the time. Weird."

"It's all good. Nice to hear from you."

"I would have called sooner but I was trying to avoid looking like a stalker," he laughed.

"Oh you should have called, you know I'm well versed in stalker and all that weird stuff. I see it all day long," she laughed playfully.

"I'm calling now though. I'm about to go for a hike and was hoping if you weren't too busy you'd consider joining me."

"Ooh a hike this early in the morning? Let me think. My body says no but my mind says yes."

"So you think we can get your mind and body to get in agreement?"

"You know what? I could use a good hike. Text me the address and I'll meet you in an hour."

"Word. This is going to be a good hike. I haven't had a walking partner in a minute now. Don't try to flake out on me either. You know I'll put a missing person bulletin out on your ass," laughed Nigel.

"I'm sure. I'll see you in a few," she giggled.

In an instant Tiffany's day had developed like film in a dark room. She jumped out the bed and ran the shower water while she laid out her clothes. She wasn't trying to be sexy but she didn't want to look homely either, so she found her cutest jade Capri yoga pants that she actually had the matching tank top to it. It was actually one of Tiffany's last purchases online for herself. She saw it on special for $25 bucks and figured it would come in handy one day. Who knew? She was right! Now all she needed was some cute tennis shoes to match. She had come too far to turn back now and she was going for total and complete cuteness. She looked in her own shoe closet and almost felt ashamed of what looked back at her. There was no way she was going to wear her clunky dirty sneakers to meet Nigel. Even if she wasn't that vain she enjoyed the chase of it all. She wanted to look good to him.

In an instant she realized that she was co-owner of one of the largest teen shoe extravaganza that belonged to her dear daughter Princess. It was just her luck that they actually wore the same shoe size at the present moment. Lord knows that was subject to change any day. The angels were looking out for Tiffany every which way because it couldn't have been more perfect that Princess was away from home which meant there was no objection to her borrowing the shoes. She retrieved the black Pumas that Princess wore maybe twice and felt good about her fitness inspired look that she pulled together. As she glanced at herself in the mirror she sensed something missing. What did her outfit need? There was some accessory she could add that wouldn't make her look like she was trying too hard. She looked through Princess many jewelry boxes and contraptions and found a cute gold tone anklet and bracelet that looked good with her ensemble.

Satisfied with her appearance Tiffany found a headband to hold her bouncy curls away from her face. She grabbed her cell phone and her pocket book and was on her way out the door for her hike with Nigel. She pulled up the address she was meeting Nigel at in her GPS on her cell phone and was guided in the direction of her new love interest. The coordinates were familiar; she had been there before. In an instant she figured it out before she could start her GPS, they were meeting at Belle Isle. It had been a while since Tiffany had last hike there but she always loved the views of the city from the bridge. It wasn't living on a grand scale but it was beautiful. The river attracted people from all over. Traffic in the parks always increased when the weather was pleasant and this day already had the makings of beautiful.

When Tiffany pulled into the parking lot on Tredegar Street she saw Nigel perched atop the hood of his black BMW looking like a black hood ornament. She chuckled to herself. He was cute but definitely different from Chris and even Will for that matter. Tiffany pulled into any empty spot three spaces down from Nigel and hopped out the car enthusiastically.

"Hey Gorgeous," said Nigel approaching her with his arms extended for a hug.

"Nigel, good to see you," she accepted his embrace.

"Thanks for meeting me last minute this morning. I could use some company today. A man gets tired of being alone you know."

"Thank you for inviting me. I really needed to get away for a minute. This hike will be good."

"That's what I'm talking about. Everything okay with your daughter?"

"Yeah everything is good. You know the regular stuff I guess," laughed Tiffany.

"Well I must say amongst it all you're looking absolutely beautiful this morning," complimented Nigel.

"Aww, that's sweet. Thanks Nigel," blushed Tiffany.

"So I stopped and got us some waters and fruit just in case we got hungry on our hike," he said grabbing the book bag out of his front passenger seat.

"How thoughtful? I was in such a rush I didn't even grab my water bottle. You're on point. I like that."

"Well I like what you like," he laughed.

"I like you Nigel," said Tiffany playfully wrapping her arms around his neck.

"Damn, I like me too. But I like you more," he said matching her flirting by wrapping his arms around her waist letting his hands just barely caress her butt.

"Lord have mercy. What am I going to do with you?" asked Tiffany as her faced warmed with excitement.

"You tell me," said Nigel sensually stroking the backside of Tiffany's forearm.

"Let's do this," Tiffany asserted with a deep laugh.

Tiffany and Nigel started their hike on a good note. Nigel was feeling Tiffany. Tiffany was feeling Nigel. It was a win win situation so far. Tiffany was enjoying how the date was unfolding. This was the first time that Tiffany had ever really considered dating another police officer. She had gone one dates with officers and even had sex with a few, she most certainly had never considered actually dating an officer. She knew firsthand how dangerous the work is, did she really want two parents for her daughter that works in law enforcement? Tiffany tried not to let her overthinking poison the good time she was already having. Instead she just tried to focus on not making too many ugly faces on this hike. That made her smile on the inside and took some of the pressure off her. It was just a hike. There was no guarantee that things would progress or develop into anything. Tiffany prayed for discernment, her judgment hadn't been bad lately but she was feeling guilt about the nature of her relationship with Chris and why she would settle for sex over a relationship. She desperately didn't want to make any mistakes with Nigel and jump into anything too soon. That meant having sex with him. That was going to be hard because even though Nigel physically was striking, she was turned on by his persona. He was coy, even charming and Tiffany ate it all up.

Halfway across the bridge the duo both stopped and pulled out their phones for the perfectly romantic selfie. In an instant that moment had been locked in history as a picture. Passersby obliged the couple their selfie moment before continuing their commute across the bridge. Their time together was fun. Tiffany laughed at his jokes because she truly thought they were funny. He liked to see the smile light up her whole face. Nigel very much felt like the man that Tiffany was missing. Impressed beyond belief Tiffany was floating on cloud nine during the drive back to her house. She couldn't remember the last time she laughed so much and truly enjoyed a man's touch that didn't involve sex. Nigel wasn't inappropriate or anything but he was affectionate. There were lots of soft caresses and touches that weren't sexual yet made her body tingle. Brunch as they called it was great and they had already made plans for dinner that evening. Tiffany was going for broke this weekend. Child free, great sex and date having weekend.

Tiffany fantasized about future dates. What their kids could look like? His penis size? What type of people his parents are? Her mind was racing a million miles a minute giving her a mild headache. She tried to relax but then got caught up trying to figure out what to wear to dinner. As she turned into her neighborhood Tiffany became startled by the police cars and their lights parked outside her friends' home. She pulled over and jumped out the car. Inside the house Tiffany found a beaten and battered Myshelle flanked by two patrolmen in the living room of her home.

"Excuse us ma'am," blocked the black officer.

"Officer Saunders sir. This is my best friend and neighbor."

The officer gave his approval nod and Tiffany ran to her friend's side.

"What happened to you?" cried Tiffany.

"It happened so fast," Myshelle stammered.

"What happened sweetie? Talk to me."

"Rod found out we went to the bar. Someone told him they saw me acting like a whore in the bar and he went off. I tried to leave but," whimpered Myshelle.

"But what?"

"He wouldn't let me leave."

"Where are the kids?"

"I sent them to my Mom's house."

"Good. They definitely don't need to be here for this."

"Where's Rod?"

"I don't know," she cried.

"I'll go see what's going on."

Tiffany spun around to the officer that approved her, "sir, where's her husband?"

"He's in the unit."

"Okay. Thanks."

Tiffany jogged outside peering inside each police cruiser till she found the one that held TyRod Covington inside. He was handcuffed seated in the back of the cruiser looking like the color red. He was fuming. He was also wreaking of alcohol this early in the day.

"Rod what's going on?" asked Tiffany.

"Get me out of this car Tiffany. Tell your boys in blue to take me out of these fucking handcuffs right now! Ain't these your people?"

"Rod you sound crazy. What's this all about?"

"You know what it's about. You took her to that bar and now my wife has been shoving some random nigga's dick down her throat for the last two weeks. Thanks Tiffany. Appreciate it."

"What?" asked Tiffany stunned.

"Don't play stupid. I know you knew. She said you took her to the bar where she met dude at. "

"Rod I took her to the bar, yes but in no way shape or form did I advocate or put her up to cheating on you. She didn't even tell me she saw him since that day at the bar."

"So you know who he is?"

"I don't know him personally but we all met. "

"You tell that pussy when I see him it's his ass. Or maybe I'll find his wife and shove my dick down her throat? Umm, yeah that sounds better. Get these handcuffs off me now Tiffany."

"Listen I want to ask them to let you go but look how you're acting. I would be mad too but how you're reacting now is just not good. So calm down so I can ask these good people to let you get your belongings and leave. "

"Please," he tried to ask nicely as calm as he could muster.

"Rod what y'all gone do after this though?"

"I don't know Tiffany. Things will never be the same again between us. But I'm going to leave. She can keep the house. I just can't go to jail. I've come too far for this."

"Let me go see what I can do. Otherwise just chill please," begged Tiffany.

"I'm trying to."

Tiffany sprinted off in the direction of the Officer in charge. She found the Sargent speaking with Myshelle. Tiffany interrupted them abruptly, "sir, can I speak to you outside please?"

"You are?"

"Officer Saunders, not my jurisdiction but this is my best friend and neighbor. I live next door," she pointed to her house.

"Outside Officer."

Tiffany followed her senior officer outside the house.

"Sir are you arresting my friend?"

"Mrs. Covington, no ma'am. She's not being charged."

"Oh yes, she's my friend too but I'm talking about her husband."

"She doesn't want to press charges but technically she doesn't have to. She's visibly beaten and battered."

"I know but sir, charges isn't going to help this situation get better. This is a family problem between a husband and his wife. Not a husband, his wife, the police department, the family court system...only because I have known both of them all my life can I assure you that there is not going to be any further incidents in this home or amongst this family tonight, tomorrow or ever. "

"You can't guarantee that if I let him loose I won't be back here in 7 hours to pick up her body, hell or his. These situations are never the same."

"Sir, these aren't those people. I make no excuses but their marriage is going through some tough stuff right now. He just found out she was cheating on him. Plus, I'm going to take Myshelle with me. She'll stay at my house until this whole thing settles down. That is my word sir."

The officer shifts his weight from one foot to the other nervously as he contemplates what to do.

"I don't like this at all. But I trust that you're a woman of your word and an Officer above all. If something should happen further I trust that you will call me directly," he commanded.

"Of course but that won't be necessary. Thank you sir. I owe you."

"You do," he said walking off.

Tiffany sprinted back inside to get Myshelle ready to go. "Myshelle, let's go honey. You're going to stay with me tonight," soothed Tiffany.

"I don't want to stay with you. I want to stay in my own house. He's going to be locked up. I'll be fine."

"See that's the thing, they aren't going to lock him up. I asked them to release him."

"You did what?"

"This is Ty we're talking about. You don't really want him to go to jail."

"Look at what he did to me. He deserves to go to jail," she whimpered.

"He was wrong for what he did. I don't support that but I also don't support extramarital affairs and things of that nature."

"How dare you throw this back on me?"

"No, you did this to yourself. And then you dragged me into it by telling him that I damn near set you up for it!"

"You took me out!"

"To get away! Not to be a whore!"

"I'm not leaving my house," screamed Myshelle.

"Yes you are. You created this mess and now I'm trying to clean it up. Regardless of how you feel, think of the embarrassment of your children, your family, or maybe even his business partners... when your husband's picture shows up in the "Gotcha" newspaper in a week or so? Stop being selfish and think about your family! The shit that's going on between you guys is foul. Truly I wish I could just step the fuck out of it and let you guys screw your own lives up but it doesn't work that way. You're my friend and he's my friend too. Your kids are my God kids and I don't want them dealing with the effects of y'alls bullshit. Now you can make this difficult for your family or you can make the best decision you've made in weeks to get your ass up, pack a bag and walk your ass next door to my house so that these officers can let your husband go. Y'all don't need this Myshelle. You know I know how you feel and if I knew you didn't really love him or care about your marriage we'd be whipping his ass together right now. That's my word!"

"I'm leaving but I'm not staying with you. Thank you Tiffany," said Myshelle getting up to pack her belongings. Tiffany hung around until Myshelle had gotten in her truck and pulled off. The last officer on the scene released the hand cuffs off TyRod who thanked him. With his head down, chin resting on his chest TyRod gave Tiffany a half hug from the side.

"Thanks fam," he said somberly.

"Thank me by ensuring this never happens again. That's not how you fix your problems Rod. Keep your hands off of her!"

He nodded in agreement and walked away. His heart felt like it had been crushed into a million tiny pieces. On top of feeling like he lost his best friend in the world, he felt like shit for losing control of his temper. There had been many nights before with angry yelling, cursing, high tensions and he had always been able to walk away no matter how many times she slapped, pushed or scratched him. He had gotten use to receiving the blunt end of his wife's anger when their arguments escalated. When Myshelle slapped him this time something snapped in him. It was definitely one of the lowest emotional points in his life, Rod was always wanting to be a source of security and protection for his wife, even if things were rocky. TyRod walked inside his house that no longer felt like a home and closed the door behind him.

Just like that her two closest friends in the world were gone in separate directions. There were so many emotions running rampant in Tiffany's mind. She did feel guilty about taking Myshelle out. Even though she didn't force Myshelle to cheat, she felt like she did. Myshelle and Rod had been through the cheating thing before. When TyRod cheated on Myshelle she stood by him. She didn't consider divorce then and Tiffany prayed that was farthest from both of her friends' minds and hearts.

Once inside her own house Tiffany checked her answering machine messages. It was mostly bill collectors and telemarketers. She sank into the couch in her den and hoped that it would swallow her up whole and whisk her off to some sort of magical couch land where real problems didn't exist. About two seconds into her attempt to relax she thought of her daughter. Tiffany retrieves her cellphone and dials her daughter's cell phone.

Princess answered almost on cue, "Hi Mom."

"Hey doll baby I miss you," gushed Tiffany.

"I miss you too Mom but I'm having a good time here. I'm coming home tomorrow though. I miss you and my room...and silence for that matter," Princess giggled.

"I miss you too sweetheart. Have you talked to Tyshelle today?"

"Yeah I heard. I feel so bad for her. She said they were arguing all day. I told her she could stay with us Sunday night so we can go to school together Monday."

"Of course. Well I'm glad you talked to her. I'm sure everything will be alright in the long run."

"Maybe. Maybe not. You know how adults are Mom."

"You are right; adults are a certain kind of way. Baby I love you. Tell everybody I said hello. I'll see you tomorrow."

"I love you too Mom. Night."

Tiffany hugged her phone as if it was her daughter. Definitely wasn't the same. As soon as she rested her phone on her chest and closed her eyes to decompress it began to ring and vibrate off her boobs into her face. Bad idea all the way around. It was Nigel. She had totally forgotten that she was supposed to be having dinner with him. It was no way she was going out but she didn't want to flake on him so she answered just before it went into her voicemail.

"Hey," said TIffany with a forced smile.

"Beautiful, thank God you answered. I thought for a second you had a change of heart," Nigel laughed.

"Oh no, stop playing. Of course I didn't change my mind but the craziest thing happened when I left you. My best friend and her husband who live next door to me had a very bad physical fight and he was being arrested when I pulled up."

"Whoa, I wasn't expecting that. I thought you might have made a stop at the store or something. I was way off. I'm sorry. Is your friend's husband in jail?" Nigel asked.

"No I was able to convince the commanding officer that the dispute was over and that they weren't going to be in the same place for the next few nights. I offered my friend to stay with me but apparently she is pissed with me because I got her husband released. She wanted him to go to jail. But I know that's not how she really feels. No one wants to see their loved ones go through what we see so much of each day on the job."

"I know. I think you did the right thing though and even if your friend can't appreciate it now, someday she will and I know he appreciates it. I'm not excusing his behavior but sometimes families can deal with their problems personally. I'll be praying for your folks' man, that's tough. So I see you're not really standing me up."

"No. I wouldn't do that to you. I was looking forward to spending more time with you. Truly I just don't think I'm the best company right now. Feeling kind of shitty truthfully."

"Why?" asked

Nigel.

"Because she met your brother that night I took her out. She's been seeing him and apparently sucking his dick every chance she can."

"What?"

"Nick. That's your brother right?"

"That most certainly is my brother but I can assure you that he has not seen your friend since that night at the bar. Nick can be fucked up but he's not cheating on his wife with your friend. He flirts a lot these days but he's trying to do the 1-woman thing. Plus, if he had he would have told me."

"What?"

"So she lied to Rod about who she was cheating with? Why would she do that?"

"I don't know but we can call my brother right now and he will tell you the same thing."

"No need, I believe you."

"That's messed up. I know you aren't even in the best mood but let me bring some Chinese over and take your mind off this shitty turn of events. I can hit up the Redbox and get us a little entertainment," Nigel offered.

"I would love to take you up on that but something just came up. I've got to get to the bottom of what lie I was pulled into tonight. I appreciate the information though. Can I call you when I get back in the house?"

"Of course I'll be up."

"Cool. I'll talk to you soon," said Tiffany hanging up quickly. She didn't even bother to call Myshelle's cell phone, she had her thoughts about where she could find her friend.

CHAPTER IV:

FROM BAD TO WORSE

Tiffany became more furious the more her conversation with Nigel played over and over in her head. It was no way Tiffany was going to play the scapegoat for Myshelle's infidelities. Maybe she wouldn't have had a problem being the fall guy if she knew that was the role she was supposed to be playing. Their sisterhood/friendship dated back decades but it all hung in the balance now. Surely their friendship had survived many tests and Tiffany hoped that clear heads would prevail. Still she was going to get an explanation tonight if she had to drive all the way across the country to get it.

Lucky for Tiffany she wouldn't have to drive that far to get her own personal justice. It was only a few places Myshelle would go under the current circumstances and clearly she wasn't at her house so that left only 1 or 2 places. The second place would be work but she definitely wasn't there because she didn't have a job. So Tiffany jumped on the highway to go to the last place she could be in Richmond, Myshelle's mother's home in the retirement community off Iron Bridge Road. It didn't take her long to get there and just as she predicted Myshelle's red truck was parked in one of her mother's assigned parking spaces. She could have called to warn her she was coming in but Tiffany favored the element of surprise not to mention she had her own key. Tiffany

unlocked the door and burst in fully mad and confrontational, "why did you lie

on me?" yelled Tiffany.

When the door swung open Tiffany almost choked on her own saliva as

she gasped in disbelief. There was Myshelle on her hands and knees with a large

yet familiar looking penis in her mouth. As Tiffany adjusted her vision and began

to squint her best friend's partner in action became very clear. It was Chris.

"Oh my," was all she could mouth.

Myshelle was so engrossed in pleasuring him that she hadn't even

noticed that she had an audience. Tiffany was mad before but now she was

disgusted. Not only had her best friend in the whole world lied to her, she

betrayed her beyond belief. Clearly Tiffany had shared too much of her personal

business with Myshelle. All that bragging must have inspired her to get her own

taste. Literally. Her first instinct was to pull out her cell phone and record the

whole sordid mess but she opted to take a picture. It was worth a thousand

words. The loud flutter and flash from the camera caught both Myshelle and

Chris's attention.

"Care to say cheese folk," smiled Tiffany as she pressed the capture

button on her cell phone rapidly over and over.

"Tiffany! What are you doing here?" screamed Myshelle in horror as she grasped for her clothes strewn all over the floor.

"Oh shit is that Tiffany for real," panicked Chris.

"Y'all keep doing what you're doing. I'm out. Good riddance," she said slamming the door behind her.

Pissed yet satisfied with the answer she got Tiffany jogged back to her car quickly to avoid any further scene. As she opened the driver side door Chris ran out half-dressed waving her down to stop. Tiffany kept rolling along unbothered by the chase but Chris was fast and physically in shape, he caught up to her and was grabbing on her car door handle before she could get out of the parking lot.

"Back up before I run your ass down," Tiffany ordered.

"Stop Tiffany. Let me explain," he pleaded.

"Explain what. That you've been playing me. Playing with my emotions and fucking my best friend at the same time."

"Stop so we can talk. Please," he begged.

The tires to the old Camry screeched to a halt. Tiffany rolled her window down just enough to let a slither of air in.

"This is messed up on so many levels. I never expected to catch you and her. Why?"

"I don't know. This hasn't been going on long. About two weeks' tops. I'm dead wrong."

"Not to me. You don't owe me anything. We aren't in a relationship. It's only my fault that I let my feelings get caught up. What's wrong with this is that you know she is a married woman. You've sat at a dinner table with her husband. How fucked up can you be?"

"I am scum for that but it wasn't personal. Rod is a good guy. It was just sex; I wasn't courting her or taking her out. She showed up at my studio wanting to work out. So I started training her. Two days in she started flirting and coming on to me. She practically begged me to have sex with her."

"And you obliged right?"

"I didn't mean to. I'm so sorry."

"It's okay. Timing is a bitch though. I thought we were about to take things to the next level."

"I know. Me too. I really never meant to screw things up with you. I love you Tiffany."

"No you definitely don't love me but I'm better off knowing now. Pass this message to Myshelle. Even though you're a sucky slutty friend I forgive you. When she's ready to woman up she should come see me."

And just like that Tiffany pulled off leaving Chris standing in the parking lot to his own thoughts. Funny how quickly things changed. She just laughed out loud. In less than 24 hours she'd lost a best friend and a lover. How unlucky could one day or person be? Out of all the men in the world, she had to choose the one she was sleeping with too. Again Tiffany blamed herself. She divulged too much to Myshelle trusting that their friendship was solid as a rock. Tiffany shared lots of the dirty sordid details of her sexual encounters completely and vividly, and all along her best friend was longing for her own opportunity.

Never again thought Tiffany to herself disgusted," lesson learned," blurted Tiffany as she watched Chris get smaller and smaller in her rearview mirror.

Back at home Tiffany spotted TyRod's truck parked in front of his house. She definitely had no plans of showing him the picture she took but she was going to give him the real deal. Her feet dragged as she walked the dreaded path to her friends literally and figuratively broken home. Tiffany might as well had chains wrapped around her feet the way she moved slowly almost as if it pained her to walk. She waited a few minutes after she knocked on the door but decided to come back later when there was no answer. He was probably getting some rest. As she turned to go back home the door opened.

"Tiffany come in," said Rod from behind the door.

"Hey I was about to leave. I figured you were sleeping," she said entering the house.

"No I'm up. Can't sleep right now."

"You gotta try though. How are the kids?"

"They are good. Ready to come back home but I haven't even talked to her yet so I don't know what we're going to do," he sobbed into his hands. He braced himself on the custom designed island he built for their kitchen years ago. Tiffany consoled her friend by rubbing his back gently as he cried into his palms.

"I have no right to be mad at my wife for what she did. You and I both know that I've been wrong too many times to count but this shit hurts. Why would she do that to me? To us? Our children? Why now? Everything was going good. I bought her that nice truck because she wanted it."

"I don't know. I can't imagine what she was thinking. I'm just so sorry you guys are going through this."

"Have you talked to her?"

"Not really. I came by to tell you what I found out."

"Which is?"

"She's not cheating with the guy Nick she met with me at the bar. I'm seeing his brother who confirmed that his brother hasn't seen nor talked to Myshelle since that night."

"What? Why would she tell me that then?"

"To throw you off track. Send you in another direction."

"So who is she seeing?"

"Before I tell you, you must make me a promise," she advised.

"What?"

"That you won't do anything criminal."

"Who is it?" he fumed.

"Chris."

"The guy you're fucking?" he asked confused.

"I mean if you want to put it like that...but definitely not anymore."

"What the fuck? This man has eaten dinner in my home many times, sat on my furniture, watched ball with me. We've talked about women together, my wife included and he's fucking her. That's low. You know I'm going to kill him right?"

"No you can't do that. I didn't tell you for that reason."

"Maybe but it's not going to change the end result."

"Rod you got to get yourself together. The police were just here yesterday, hell last night. You know I don't condone what you did to her. She's truly fucked up for doing this to you especially to have forgiven you for the same thing but she didn't deserve to be beaten, fought or whatever happened. I pass no judgements but you're a grown ass man Rod, she's your wife. You two have got to figure this stuff out peacefully and civilly because I don't want to see anyone else get further hurt. I will lock you up, her, whoever if it will protect you both from doing something stupid that could fuck up your family forever. You're better than that. Don't take her back, do take her back. Just don't touch Chris. Stay away from him."

"Yeah I hear you."

"Good. I'm going home. If you need me call me."

"Tiff, how you find out?"

"It doesn't matter."

"It does to me."

"I love you man, keep your head up. You're bigger than this."

Rod walked up on Tiffany leaving barely any space between them and looked her straight in the eye, "you caught them in the act?"

Tiffany turned her head away so he wouldn't see her eyes water when she responded.

"No, what would make you say that?" she asked.

"I already know. Damn, dirty bitch," he fumed throwing the empty vase that sat on a nearby table into the wall.

"Rod, don't!"

"Damn, where? Please don't say the hotel? Not just a dirty bitch, a skank ho," he chuckled.

"It wasn't at a hotel. I don't think it matters."

"You damn sure right about that. It doesn't matter. My marriage is over. At least the kids are older now," he reasoned.

"You don't mean that."

"I wish I didn't mean it."

"Everything takes time Rod. Have faith."

"Faith isn't going to help me forget the image of my wife on her knees braining Chris up."

"Yes it will. Just believe. I'll talk to you later," said Tiffany exiting the almost never quiet Covington house. It felt eerie almost as if somebody died. Crossing the property line to her own house never felt so good. The overwhelming feeling of love, hospitality and family had evaporated from the Covington household atmosphere almost instantly. It was just a house and no longer a home. The sun didn't even seem to shine as bright. Another family, albeit a black family hanging by a thread.

Tiffany had to shift her focus to something else. She was ready for Princess to come home. She missed her baby girl. Tiffany picked up the cordless phone from the kitchen counter and dialed the number to Will's house.

"Hello," sang the cheery voice almost in a sing song manner.

"Cindy, hi," blurted Tiffany.

"Tiffany! It's been so long, how are you?" asked Cindy Knoll, Will's wife.

"I'm good. How are you doing?"

"Just wonderful darling. God is so good to me! You know we've enjoyed having Princess around. Thank you for encouraging Will to step up and be a better father to her. She is an amazing young woman and I just feel so blessed to have her in our lives. Her siblings look up to her already. I know you are one proud momma."

"That's great. I'm really glad to hear that. Thank you, I am proud of her. She's a good girl...that's why I'm calling. I miss my baby. Can I speak to her please?"

"Aww I bet you do. She talks about you all the time. Let me see if I can find her really quick," said Cindy.

"Thanks."

Cindy presses the intercom button on the console panel mounted on the wall of her bedroom, "Princess your mom is on the phone. Pick up please."

There is silence.

"It should only be a minute. She's in here somewhere. How about this? Let me get up off my butt and go find her and I'll have her call you right back."

"Okay. Good talking to you Cindy."

"Likewise Tiffany. You're going to join us for dinner soon right?"

"Of course, just let me know."

"Yes ma'am. I sure will. Bye bye."

"Bye," chimed Tiffany back at Cindy.

That was a positive and friendly conversation. Maybe Cindy had changed too. If things were going to be like this between them, it would definitely be a better experience this time around having them back in their lives. Maybe time does heal. People mature. That gave Tiffany hope that one day she would be friends with Myshelle again. She didn't know when or what it would take but at least she could be hopeful. Tiffany started cleaning up the house when she lost track of time. It had been almost two hours since she had called to speak with Princess. She picked up her cordless phone and dialed Will's house number again.

"Tiffany," answered Cindy quickly.

"Hey, Prin never called me back."

"I know. I haven't been able to find her. I've been all over the house at least 10 times now. I've called her phone, the church and her friend...Tyeshelle. No one has seen her or spoken with her."

"What?" panicked Tiffany.

"I know how that sounds but she's got to be somewhere. I just saw her a few hours ago. She didn't say she was going anywhere or leaving," explained Cindy.

"That's not like her. Oh my God. Where's Will?"

"Will had a meeting out of town today."

"Have you talked to him?"

"No, he doesn't like being disturbed during his meetings."

"Call him and find out if Princess went with him now."

"Okay."

"Call me right back."

Tiffany tried to reason with herself. Princess was somewhere not paying attention to her phone. Or maybe the phone was dead and she couldn't receive calls. She wasn't even considering that something was actually very wrong as she waited for the phone to ring. Seconds later it did.

"Yes, what he say?" asked Tiffany.

"No, she's not with him. He's worried though. He's on his way home."

"What? Why is he worried?"

"He said that he wanted to call you to talk to you but he hadn't had a chance. He found some text messages in Princess phone between her and a guy that were sexual. He said he talked to Princess who said that she wasn't sexually active, just flirting."

"What? When did all of this happen?"

"Yesterday."

"What? I check her phone weekly."

"These were new texts so apparently this started when she got to our house."

"But you said she was doing good? I'm confused."

"Tiffany I had no idea. I just found out too. She has been great around me. I didn't feel like she was trying to be sneaky around me."

"So she could be with this boy... I'm on my way."

And just like that Tiffany was back in her car speeding across town. She could sure use a patrol car right now. She would fly through this traffic with the lights and sirens. Tiffany tried to stay calm but her gut was telling her that something was wrong. If Princess had been trying to be sneaky and do something at her father's house; she wouldn't not answer her cellphone. Nor would she let her cell phone die.

Tiffany tried not to be in awe as she drove up the long stretch of beautifully landscaped driveway that led to Will and Cindy's house. They had done work on the house and even added a wing since she had last visited them. It looked spectacular. Tiffany imagined Princess had been living it up with her father. Her daughter deserved it though, so Tiffany was glad that all of this beauty and splendor was now a part of her life.

Cindy was waiting in the driveway when Tiffany pulled up. They hugged quickly and rushed inside the house where Cindy escorted Tiffany to Princess's bedroom. Tiffany was taken back by her daughter's bedroom. The large room had to be to be the size of a Master bedroom. It was huge and beautifully decorated in cheerful shades of yellow, Princess's favorite color. The room look like it existed for years, not the weekend Princess had reconnected with her father.

For a moment Tiffany felt inadequate in the sense that this room was the room she would have dreamed about giving her only daughter. She had her own flat screen tv mounted in front of her queen size canopy bed draped in mosquito net and white rope lights. There was a beautiful wood desk with a lap top on it. There were pictures of Princess all over her room. Tiffany was impressed but confused at the same time. Where was her daughter?

Tiffany snapped out of her daydream and sat down at the desk and turned the computer on. Thankfully it wasn't password protected so she was able to log in quickly and peruse what her daughter had been getting into while away from home. Tiffany clicked on the GMAIL icon, the inbox of a teen girl...a wonderful thing. Princess had all sorts of emails, some personal. Some school related. Mostly sales alerts and social media updates. Not satisfied Tiffany clicked on the deleted messages icon. The last email was from Justin that read:

"Hey Princess. I called u last night. No answer, waz up with that? We still on for later?"

Tiffany forwarded the email to her personal email account just in case she needed to get in contact with Justin later. She then clicked on the Facebook icon. Princess had several notifications but no new posts or updates to her personal page in two days. That was strange thought Tiffany. Her daughter was famous for posting anything and everything. It wasn't exactly like her to go days without posting anything. She tried to reason with herself that she was worrying for nothing. Her daughter was having a good time somewhere cringing that she would probably be in trouble for being unreachable. Still Tiffany continued looking for clues around her daughter's bedroom when Cindy walked in followed by Will's younger daughter Jymeshia.

"Tiffany, Jymeshia said she overhead Princess on the phone this morning. Tell her what you heard," ordered Cindy.

"Well Princess was telling somebody that she was coming to their house. She was whispering and trying to not be heard but I was being nosey so I kept trying to listen. She said something about shots and smoke, then she hung up and left in a hurry."

"Shots and smoke? Princess doesn't drink or smoke. Thanks, you wouldn't happen to have heard where she was going?"

"No ma'am. I followed her outside and asked her when she was coming back. She just said later. There was a car waiting for her outside the driveway."

"What kind of car?" asked Tiffany, more puzzled than before.

"I don't know but it was black and fancy."

"I know I'm pushing it but did you see the license plate?"

"No...I didn't think to get the plates. I'm sorry Tiffany."

"Sorry for what. You did good. This helps a lot. Thank you. You are all grown up now! So pretty too," said Tiffany hugging her daughter's sister from another woman.

"I'm sure she okay though. Princess is too smart to get herself into any trouble," offered Jymeshia.

"You're probably right. If you hear from her please tell her to call me and her Dad ASAP."

"Yes ma'am. Princess said I could spend the night with y'all soon?"

"Yes ma'am, anytime."

"Yay, wait till she gets back. I can't wait to tell her."

"Mesh, go help Louise in the kitchen, she's preparing dinner."

"Yes ma'am," said Jymeshia running off obediently.

Tiffany pulled out her cell phone and dialed her daughter's number again. It rang and rang and eventually went into the voicemail.

"Princess you're not in trouble yet. I'm at your father's house with Cindy. Please call me immediately so we can know you are safe. Love you baby."

Tiffany hung up still feeling like something was wrong. Something was gnawing at her soul telling her she should be scared. She just broke down in tears crying. Cindy tried to console her.

"Aww, sweetie please don't cry. You know how these kids are. Princess is a good kid. She's okay I promise. Come on let's go sit in the den. We can wait for her in there," said Cindy helping Tiffany out the room.

Exhausted, drained and scared Tiffany almost dropped into the leather sectional lifeless with no energy. Cindy helped her prop her feet up and then retrieved a glass of lemonade from the kitchen for her. "Drink this Tiff."

"Thanks, I'm trying to not think of the worst but the officer in me keeps telling me otherwise."

"I hear you. God wouldn't let anything happen to our girl. No, he wouldn't. I'm going to help Louise finish up this dinner. Please don't move. Relax. Mi casa es su casa."

"Thanks Cindy," said Tiffany sipping the cold sweet beverage.

Tiffany tried to watch the embroiling matters on CNN but her mind kept drifting back to her daughter. She looked at her phone repeatedly. No calls, no text messages, emails. Nothing. At some point Tiffany must have dozed off because she woke up covered in a blanket in panic.

"What time is it?" she blurted to no one.

Louise, the cook overheard her and peaked her head out the kitchen, "almost 9."

"What? Prin still not here?"

Tiffany pulled out her cell phone again and dialed her daughter's number. This time it went straight into voicemail without ringing. She hung up and dialed Tyshelle's number.

"Hey auntie," said Tyshelle.

"Hey baby. Please tell me you have heard from Prin?"

"Not since yesterday."

"No texts or nothing?"

"Nope and I was just starting to wonder what was up with her."

"Oh my God. Where is she?"

"Did you call Justin? She might be with him?"

"I don't have his number. Just his email."

"His number is 804-665-3294."

"Thanks Ty, I'll call you back."

Tiffany hung up and dialed the number.

"Who dis?" asked a brazen boys voice.

"Dis is Princess's mother. Is my daughter with you?"

"My bad. No ma'am. I haven't seen Princess since she got picked up from my house earlier."

"What?"

"I picked her up today from her father's house to come over and study. She was here an hour tops, then her phone started ringing and buzzing off the hook and she left. I've been calling her all evening. She won't answer for me."

"Did something happen between you two today?"

"No ma'am. I would never try anything with Princess. I know you're a cop!"

"What kind of car did you pick her up in Justin?"

"My mom's black Benz. Please don't tell her though, she has no idea I drove it."

"Okay Justin. Thanks for the information. If you hear from her, tell her I'm looking for her. By any chance did you happen to see what kind of car she left in?"

"Yes ma'am. Or should I say, Officer?" he asked dumbfounded.

"Ma'am is fine. Did you see who picked her up Justin?" quizzed Tiffany.

"No by the time I got to the door she was gone. Like she vanished into thin air. I thought she was playing some sort of game or something."

"Thanks Justin. If you hear something, please call me immediately."

"Yes ma'am."

"Good night."

"Night ma'am."

Tiffany ended the call fully convinced something was wrong now. She found Cindy in the laundry room folding clothes.

"You're awake?" asked Cindy startled.

"Yeah I'm about to head to the precinct. I just talked to Justin who picked her up to study earlier today."

"Great where is she then?"

"No clue. He said she got picked up at his house almost an hour into their study date."

"Will should be here soon. He said he's about 30 minutes away."

"Tell him to meet me at my precinct."

"Okay. Call me if you hear anything."

"Likewise?"

"Yes, I will call you if she shows up or calls."

"Bye," said Tiffany sadly as she raced to her car and sped off into the night.

Lord, where could Princess be? Tiffany's mind wandered incessantly about the whereabouts of her daughter.

CHAPTER V:

FEAR AND FAITH

Tiffany tried to breathe but it felt as if her chest was caving in with every breath she took, it was getting tighter. She clutched her chest for dear mercy but there was no relief of the excruciating pain she was experiencing. Tiffany felt like she was having a heart attack when it was probably more of an anxiety or panic attack.

"Calm down Tiffany. I know this seems really bad but I'm trusting that God wouldn't let anything happen to our daughter. You have to trust God right now," said Will trying to console her.

Tiffany struggled, the words wouldn't come out.

"It's okay, shh..don't say anything. Just sit down and relax."

Will pulled out the chair from the conference room table within the Grace Street precinct where Tiffany worked so she could get off her feet.

"I just don't understand why she wouldn't have called or text one of us by now. My gut feeling is telling me something is wrong. My baby wouldn't just be missing for this long," cried Tiffany.

"No, let's not rush to assumptions Tiffany. Maybe she's God knows where doing God knows what! She is a teenager. You know how unpredictable teens can be."

"True but this just doesn't feel right. It's this unsettling feeling in the pit of my stomach telling me that I should be out searching for our daughter."

There was a knock on the door that interrupted Will's pragmatic response to the mother of his child.

"Come in," replied Tiffany.

In walked Tiffany's old partner Jeff Hustis, a well-dressed and well liked white detective. Jeff and Tiffany were partners back in their early patrol days. They both had been promoted to their respective positions in different departments but they still remained close friends. He walked straight over to Tiffany and embraced her with the biggest hug he could give her.

"Hey Jeff," said Tiffany embracing him tightly.

"Hey doll. I just heard. What you need me to do?"

"I don't know honestly. I've given them everything they need to get her information entered into system. An Amber Alert would be nice but from what I hear that is in motion."

"In motion? Bullshit…they better get it done."

"I know. I'm just scared."

"Don't be Tiffany. We're going to tear these streets apart until we find her. That's my word."

"I pray it doesn't have to get that deep."

"Yeah but whatever it takes. That's my boo too you know."

"I know," smiled Tiffany.

"Why are you here? Go home. So you can be there if she shows up."

"I can't. It's going to drive me crazy…Lord, where are my manners? Jeff, this is Princess father Will. Will, this is my old partner and friend for life Jeff."

Will extended his hand to shake Jeff's, "Nice to meet you."

"Likewise," nodded Jeff in agreement.

"So when was she last seen or heard from?" inquired Jeff.

"She was staying at her father's house when she went to study with a classmate named Justin. He says that she was at his house for an hour before she was picked up."

"Did he get a license plate?"

"Of course not. He didn't see the vehicle she left in."

"You got his address?"

"Yeah."

"Text it to me right now. I'm going to send a couple of guys over to check him out. Maybe there's a surveillance camera somewhere in the area that may have gotten the license plates of the vehicle she left in and who she left with."

"Thanks Jeff."

"It's nothing. Shoot me that text now so I can go grab a couple guys to get on it ASAP."

Tiffany pulled out her phone and text the address to Jeff as he requested.

"Please call me as soon as you know something."

"I got you. Get out of here though. You don't need to be in here right now. I'll talk to your Captain and explain what's going on."

"Okay," she said taking a deep breath.

"You know we're not going to let anything happen to our baby girl?"

"I know; I just pray nothing has happened to her yet."

"Don't even think like that. Will, nice meeting you again sir, sorry it's under these circumstances but rest assured everyone at this precinct has watched your daughter grow up and love her like she's our own kid. We won't stop until she's back home safe and sound."

"Thank you," said Will.

"Now do me a solid and get her out of here please."

"I don't want to be kicked out," pleaded Tiffany lying her head on the conference room table and gripping it for dear life.

"Let's go Tiffany. You can come back to my house with us. You don't need to be alone."

Tiffany reluctantly got up from her seat not wanting to move but knowing there was nothing she was truly going to accomplish by sitting in the conference room pondering the whereabouts of her daughter.

"As soon as I hear something I'll either call or come by, okay?" reassured Jeff.

"Thanks," Tiffany managed to whisper.

Downstairs in the parking deck Tiffany and Will hugged as they stood next to their respective vehicles.

"It's going to be alright," Will offered.

"I pray so."

"You coming back to my house with us?"

"Thanks for the offer but I'd rather go home. You know if I hear anything I'll call you."

"Okay."

Tiffany climbed into the driver seat of her car, worn and weary. She prayed that by some miracle she would walk in her house and her daughter would be sitting on the couch watching television oblivious to the sheer panic she was experiencing. When Tiffany got home there was no such luck. There were no indications that Princess had been home. No calls, messages, emails. Nothing. Her daughter's phone still rang busy. She could feel the tension trying to almost smother her, so she tried to breath.

Just as she was about to lay down her doorbell began to ring. She jumped up anxious and excited that her daughter had returned home. Hell she must have lost her keys and her phone. Glory to God Tiffany thought as she ran down the stairs and flung open the front door.

"Prin...", she exclaimed before fully focusing on the figure standing before her. It was Myshelle.

"Oh it's just you," Tiffany said shutting the door in her best friends face and walking back into her living room.

Myshelle opened the door, locked it behind her and followed her now estranged friend to her living room.

"I'm not even going to say anything because I deserve that."

"Bitch you deserve a lot more but I'm too much of a woman and a police officer to do it."

"I didn't come here for this Tiffany. I came here to check on my God daughter."

"Oh well excuse the hell out of me. How bold of you!"

"I know you're mad. You have every right to be. What can I say? I'm sorry. I was in a bad place Tiffany. My marriage is lackluster at best. I didn't mean to hurt you."

"Well that's mighty white of you to apologize yet you didn't come here for this!"

"Can we ever get pass this and be friends again?"

"I don't care about our friendship and neither did you when you were on your knees orally pleasuring the man that I care about and love."

"You weren't even together!"

"Some things take time! And last time I checked. You're married. It's none of your business. Your business is TyRod Covington...your husband."

"Rod and I are over."

"What?"

"I can't do it anymore Tiff. He's just not the man I need."

"You sound like a fool!"

"What?"

"I said it. You sound stupid! He's not the man you need. So you don't need a man that loves you, your children and your family. He works hard to provide for you all. Would do anything for you and your kids? You right, I don't know who needs that type of man! Whew," said Tiffany sarcastically.

"Of course those are the things that make him great but I need more than just a provider and a good father. I need a good husband. A Lover and friend," explained Myshelle.

"And Chris was that?"

"No, that was sex. Chris and I are just friends who never should have crossed that line. I realize that now. It was my fault. I threw myself at him and made it very hard for him to say no. I know I was wrong and I'm sorry for it. We haven't seen each other since you caught us. He won't return my calls or my texts."

"So that's what it really is? He cut you slam off!"

"Yes...no! Even if he did answer my calls the fling is over. He loves you. He's pissed that we hurt you and now he's lost you."

"Well thank you for sharing that. I accept your apology. I even forgive you for being a ratchet chick but our friendship will never be the same again."

Myshelle starts to cry and sob uncontrollably, "I hurt the people that matter the most to me. I never intended to hurt you, Rod, our children."

"I wish I could say I feel sorry for you but you are the composer of your own little sinful symphony."

"What an analogy Tiffany," chuckled Myshelle through her tears.

"That was good," Tiffany confirmed.

"Look I know all things take time. I realize that but I can't imagine losing my friend, hell my sister forever."

"I'm not going to lie to you. I can't even begin to focus on our friendship right now because my mind is on Prin. My baby hasn't been seen or heard from since this morning. I'm trying not to lose my mind."

"I know, that's why I came. Tyshelle told me. I almost got mad that you didn't call me or text me earlier so I could help look or do something and then I thought to myself, why would she call me?"

"Yeah I wasn't about to do that. I didn't count on seeing you for days, weeks, months, hell maybe years."

"I understand."

"What I will say is that I would never let Chris or any man, come between our friendship. Even though I'm pissed, hurt... and feel betrayed by you two. You may have done me a favor by allowing me to see that Chris wasn't good for me. He may have been good to screw but a relationship with him may have been more trouble than I need in my life."

"What can I do though? Seriously, should we be out looking for her? Knocking on doors, hell knocking heads together?" asked Myshelle.

"Nothing at this moment. I filed the missing person's report earlier so they should be releasing an Amber Alert soon. Jeff is getting someone to check out Justin again. Maybe someone has a surveillance camera in the neighborhood that recorded the vehicle Prin left in."

"This is scary. That's not like Princess at all. I'm not trying to freak you out or anything but I have a bad feeling about this Tiff. I wouldn't wait on your buddies at the precinct. You and I both know you need to get your ears to the street and see what you can find out," blurted Myshelle.

"It's not just you. I've been having the worse gnawing feeling in my heart but I'm trying not to jump to conclusions. What if she is just doing something she don't have no business doing and scared to come home? I've been hard on her and I pray that hasn't made her feel like she had to act out or do something stupid...Lord where is my child," broke down Tiffany.

Myshelle ran to console her best friend as she slumped onto the ground almost lifeless.

"Aww baby don't do that. I'm sorry...I didn't mean to scare you Tiffany. I'm just worried. Please hold it together. You've got to stay strong. Fuck how it sounds, it's real. There's a good chance nothing is wrong and Princess is fine. Or there's a possibility that something fucked up happened? The Tiffany I know wouldn't be sitting here waiting on anybody," proclaimed Myshelle.

"I know I just feel stuck...like my legs won't move. My mind is all over the place. I'm having a hard time focusing."

"Snap out of it Tiff. Your baby needs you!"

"You're right. Let's go," agreed Tiffany grabbing her cell phone and pocketbook off the dining room table.

"That's my girl. We can take my car."

"Good. I don't have gas anyway," Tiffany sobbed.

"It's all good. I got your back."

The ride to Justin's was quick and quiet. Tiffany's nerves were on full throttle because she knew what she had to do. As much as she didn't want to, she couldn't afford to allow too much more time to pass before she had some idea what happened to her daughter.

Myshelle pulled into the driveway behind several expensive luxury cars including a black Benz, presumably the last car Princess was actually seen in. Tiffany walked straight up to the front door and began to knock loudly and hurriedly on the doors. The double doors swung open and the goofiest, tallest 16-year-old high school Junior, Justin was surprised by the two women pushing through his front door into his foyer.

"You know who I am?" asked Tiffany stabbing Justin in the chest with her forefinger.

"Yes ma'am, you're Princess' mom," Justin stammered.

"Where are your parents?" asked Tiffany looking around the home for other occupants.

"I'm here alone. My parents are away in Williamsburg at a resort. I wasn't supposed to have anybody over much less drive the Benz but I really like your daughter ma'am. I just wanted to impress her."

"What makes you think you could impress my daughter with your things?"

"No, not like I was bragging or anything. I just wanted her to see that I come from a good family."

"Yeah sure."

"I swear. I wouldn't lie to you ma'am. I know you're a police officer and I also know that you're not going to let any old thug take your daughter out. Which I can totally respect."

"Maybe I believe you. Who do you think was texting her? Did she say?"

"No, she was startled by it almost. I asked her if she had to leave and she didn't even answer me. She just got up and left."

"Do your parents have surveillance camera's?" inquired Tiffany.

"Of course."

"Why didn't you tell me that earlier?" yelled Tiffany.

Myshelle popped Justin upside his forehead.

"Hey, she can't hit me," he whined.

"Who's going to arrest her?" asked Tiffany.

"Good point. I'm sorry I didn't think about it earlier. I've got to be honest. This has never happened to me. A chick just up and leave on me, no bye, explanation or anything. My confidence has just suffered a major blow," he murmured.

"Focus Justin," ordered Tiffany impatiently.

"See that's why I couldn't remember the surveillance earlier. A brotha all in his feelings and what not. Your daughter is a heartbreaker."

Myshelle popped Justin upside his head again, harder than the last time.

"Ouch," he flinched.

"It's going to get worse for you Justin if you don't get real clear about what resources we have available to aid in locating my daughter," threatened Tiffany.

"Yes ma'am, I'll be glad to pull up the footage for you. Just let me get my cell phone."

"Where is it?" asked Myshelle.

Justin pointed to the coffee table.

"Don't move," said Tiffany reaching for his phone first.

He had a way expensive fancy I Phone 6 just like her daughters. Of course like a typical teen he had a password lock on his device.

"Unlock it now," commanded Tiffany holding the phone up for him

Justin complied by putting in his four digit pass code to unlock his cell phone. Tiffany and Myshelle looked through his text messages, emails, contacts and pictures before returning his phone to him.

"I don't know how I feel about all of this," said Justin.

"Pull up the surveillance footage now. Feelings are not required," Tiffany reassured.

Justin pulled up the surveillance video app on his phone and began to rewind the footage for several cameras back to the timeframe when Princess would have left his house. He was able to pull up one image that only showed a corner of a vehicle, not a full view. It could have been any dark looking vehicle. The vehicle Princess had to leave in was never fully seen in any frame of the surveillance footage.

"Damn," lashed out Tiffany.

"I'm sorry ma'am. Maybe my neighbor across the street has cameras and got a shot of the car. I can walk you across and introduce you," offered Justin.

"Yes, you can do that. Let's go."

The three unlikely partners walked across the street to Justin's neighbor's house.

"This is Miss Fields house," advised Justin.

"Like the cookies?" asked Myshelle.

"Huh?"

"You've never heard of Miss Field's cookies?" asked Myshelle curiously.

"No, I don't eat a lot of junk," explained Justin.

"Focus people," snapped Tiffany.

"Sorry I have a mild case of ADHD. I didn't take my medicine today," confessed Justin.

"You're doing good Justin. If your parents were here, they would be proud of you."

"Thanks ma'am," he stammered as they approached Miss Field's front door. Justin pushed the doorbell and took a step back.

While they waited on someone to answer the door Tiffany was smacked in the face with a burning question?

"Justin, has any officer been here prior today?" asked Tiffany.

"No ma'am."

Waiting on Miss Fields Tiffany pondered why no one from her precinct had been by to question Justin. She filed her missing person's report for Princess hours earlier. Just as Tiffany was about to lose patience the doors swung open slowly. Miss Fields was a small stature black lady with long beautiful gray hair braided down her back.

"Who's there?" she asked squinting in the sunlight.

"It's me Miss Fields. Justin."

"Hey baby. I should have known it was you. Come on in," welcomed Miss Fields happily.

"Thanks, I'm sorry to bother you but I wanted to see if you could be of help to my friends' mother."

"What you need baby?"

"Well this is Officer Saunders, the mother of a friend of mine who is missing. She was picked up from my house earlier but no one has seen or heard from her since I saw her last. My surveillance camera didn't show the car at all. We were hoping you have cameras?"

"Of course I do. You can't trust nobody these days? Let me find my tablet and I'll pull it up for you. Have a seat in there," she pointed as she walked off to retrieve her tablet.

Justin, Myshelle and Tiffany followed instructions and sat down in the beautiful grand living room. There was a beautiful white fancy piano on a bear skin fur looking rug. Miss Fields was living large and it showed in the dressings and drapery of the room. It was magnificent on so many levels. She had better have surveillance cameras thought Tiffany as she sank into the soft cushiony charcoal sofa. There were beautiful lime green patterned pillows lined neatly down the chair.

"I'm going to go ahead and ask what everybody else is thinking," said Myshelle in amazement.

"You think this is the real Miss Fields?" Tiffany shook her head in disbelief.

"Yes!"

"No way it's her. What are the chances? Stay focused."

"I'm going to ask her."

"Myshelle please don't ask this lady that. Let me get this video footage and leave."

Justin laughed as the two best friends bickered about the legitimacy of whether they were in the home of the Miss Fields cookie phenom. When Miss Fields emerged from the other room she was carrying a tray of chocolate cookies and an I Pad.

"Get the fudge out of here?" gasped Myshelle.

"Now that's just random."

"You guys are hilarious but shouldn't we be focused on this footage," asked Justin.

Miss Fields interrupted them by setting the tray down on the table in front of the sofa. "Will you all have some cookies?" she asked sweetly.

"Of course I will. How kind of you Miss Fields!" said Myshelle sarcastically as if to prove her theory.

"No thank you. I don't even have an appetite. I'm Officer Tiffany Saunders and I'm here because my 16-year-old daughter is missing. She was last at Justin's house when she was possibly picked up by someone. I'm praying your surveillance cameras may have recorded her leaving and could shed some light on who my daughter could possibly be with," explained Tiffany.

"I see. I'm sorry. I'll do anything I can to help you find your daughter. How unfortunate? Yes, let's pull the surveillance video up," said Miss Fields as she pressed several times into her I Pad. Instantly the picture on the wall turns into a television screen.

"Justin what time did Princess leave yesterday?" asked Tiffany.

"I'm not sure exactly but I sent her a text right when she left. Let me see what time I sent it," he said pulling his phone out and going into his last text to Princess. The first one after I picked her up was at around 11:06 in the morning."

Miss Fields scrolled to her footage the day before from 9am. She scrolled through showing images of Justin driving his parents Black Benz into their driveway around the time after he picked up Princess and returned home. She scrolled further to the footage to exactly 11:01 a purple Honda Civic pulls up with Hello Kitty lashes on the headlights. The car is parked right in front of

Justin's house. Princess walks out Justin house looking down at her phone with her book bag on her shoulder. Her daughter gets into the car and it pulls off in hurry. What the video footage didn't reveal were the license plates. There is no clear shot of the front or back bumpers. It shouldn't be too hard to track down a purple Honda Civic with lashes. It clearly was a girls' car but then again in these times Tiffany knew not to draw too much into anything.

"Is there any way you can make me a copy of this and email it to me?" asked Tiffany.

"Sure, just give me your email address."

OfficerTiff@omail.com.

"I just sent the whole day of footage to you. I pray you find your daughter safe. If there's anything more I can do, please let me know."

"Yes ma'am, thank you for everything," replied Tiffany.

"You are most certainly welcome but please take some of these cookies to go. I've got much too many," she offered again.

"Thank you Miss Fields," said Myshelle grabbing a large napkin full of cookies.

"Justin tell your parents I said hello," she said as her unexpected guests left.

"Yes ma'am," he charmed.

"Thank you again. Have a good evening," said Tiffany.

When they got to the sidewalk in front of Justin's house Tiffany's mental light bulb went off again.

"Justin does someone at your school drive a car like that?"

"No. I've never seen that car before."

"Okay well thanks for everything," she said as they walked back to Myshelle's red Range Rover.

"I told you that was her," said Myshelle matter of factly.

"Whatever. I seriously doubt that was the real Miss Fields. That's some old lady that gets her kicks out of making bozos like us think that she's the real Miss Fields because she is wealthy and offered us cookies."

"Seems like a good reason to believe she is."

"The chips have gone to your head. Let's go back to my precinct. I want to look this car up in DMV."

"Why don't you just call it in?" Myshelle asked.

"Security measures," explained Tiffany.

CHAPTER VI:

WHEN LIFE GIVES YOU LEMONS; JUICE'EM

Tiffany made good use of her brief time at her precinct. She managed to find a purple Honda Civic registered to a high school student by the name of Shalonda Eubanks. Miss Eubanks was a student at Lee Davis High School with a public Facebook profile and an Instagram account that bordered on vain self-promotion at its best. They tried not to rush to judge but a picture was worth a thousand words.

Immediately Tiffany began to question how her daughter became linked up with this young lady and where were they now. The registered address of the car was a residence in Mechanicsville. That was their next stop. When they pulled onto the gravel road Tiffany became somewhat uneasy. The road was winding through the land surrounded by large trees. There was an older log cabin style home that sat back deep into the land. Dogs could be heard barking around them though they couldn't physically see where they were located. Tiffany presumed they were hunting dogs possibly in cages. She certainly was going to find out when she got out of the safety of the vehicle.

Tiffany jumped out with one hand on her weapon. There were old farm trucks and equipment but no purple Honda Civic. Tiffany walked towards the front door when someone fired a shot in the air from behind them. Startled they both jumped and turned to face the direction of the shot. Approaching them was an old white bearded black man wearing a dirty mechanics jumper. The name tag simply said Roy though it was long ago the color white.

"Whatchu' doing here on my property?" he asked bearing his shot gun.

"I'm looking for Shalonda Eubanks. I'm a police officer," said Tiffany retrieving her badge from her pocket and holding it out for his investigation.

"Sorry bout that Officer, sometimes my granddaughter's friends can be disrespectful and troublesome. You ladies look awfully young," he smiled revealing his missing teeth.

"No sir, we understand. I'm Officer Tiffany Saunders of Richmond Police Department. This is my friend Myshelle. Today I recovered surveillance footage of the purple Honda Civic registered to Shalonda Eubanks picking up my daughter from a residence in the city. My daughter hasn't been seen or heard from since she was last seen getting in this car. Is Miss Eubanks your granddaughter?" inquired Tiffany.

"Yes ma'am. Is she in trouble?"

"Not at this time. My main goal is to locate my daughter safely. I'm here unofficially if you know what I mean."

"I do," he nodded.

"Is Shalonda here?"

"No ma'am this life doesn't suit her too well. I haven't seen Shalonda in at least 3 weeks. She stops in every now and again to get some money or food. Whatever she need, then she back out there in the world as I call it."

"I see. Do you have a telephone number for her?"

"Yes, give me a second," he said pulling his cell phone out his back pocket and scrolling through his contact list.

"I told you everybody has a cell phone these days," whispered Myshelle.

"Oh I only keep this thing for her to call me when she in trouble. Who else need to talk to me? My house paid for. My truck paid for. I hunts my food. My well provides enough water or the lake down yonder. I don't need to talk to no one but I try to be available for her."

"Yes sir. May I get her number?"

Yeah, it's 8 – 0 – 4…9 – 2-2-4-1-2-3."

"Thank you," said Tiffany dialing the number in her cell phone. She hit the call button and the phone just rang and rang before the voicemail picked up. The mailbox was full. Tiffany text a message to Shalonda asking her to call her back immediately.

"Would you ladies like to come in and have a beverage or snack?" he politely offered.

"How nice of you? We actually just had Miss Field's cookies a few minutes ago. Appreciate it though," said Tiffany coolly.

"What type of trouble does your granddaughter normally get into?" asked Myshelle curiously.

"Stealing mostly. I try to give her as much money as I can but it's never enough. She lives kind of fast."

"I checked in our system, she didn't have prior charges. How could that be if she's been caught stealing?"

"She's never been arrested though. I usually pick her up from the precinct and bring her back here with me. She'll stick around long enough to get her car back and then she's back out on the road again."

"Okay. What precinct do you pick her up from?" Tiffany asked stunned by what she just learned.

"Grace Street in the city."

"That's my precinct. Is there a particular officer your granddaughter knows?"

"I don't know. She's always standing out front when I pick her up. I've never had to go inside."

"Interesting," said Tiffany and Myshelle together.

"If you hear from your granddaughter please call me," advised Tiffany handing him one of her cards.

"Certainly Officer."

Tiffany was surely stumped by the recent information. Clearly his granddaughter was some sort of criminal who was managing to avoid prosecution. She speculated about who in her own precinct was helping Miss Eubanks and for what reason. There was definitely something questionable happening right underneath her nose and now it looked like it involved her daughter. Tiffany was on to something.

"Where to now?" asked Myshelle.

"I don't know. I have no idea even where to begin looking for this chick."

"Maybe you should ask her grandfather if she has a bedroom? He'd probably let you check it."

"Good idea. You wait in the car, I'll go look. If something happens honk the horn."

"Gotcha!"

Tiffany exited the SUV to see what clues she could find about Shalonda's possible whereabouts.

"Sir, I'm sorry to bother you again but does she have a room here?"

"Yes ma'am. You can look around if you like," he offered.

"Yes sir that may help."

"Come on inside. He pulled the screen door open and walked in extending it open behind him for Tiffany. She followed him through the small cabin to a room no bigger than her bathroom at home that had a twin mattress on the floor. A huge old floor model television and lots of clothes and cigarette butts covered the floor. Tiffany sifted through the contents of the room. It certainly had character but no real clues other than she was a heavy smoker who loved lipsticks of all shades and very scantily dressed clothing. It looked like the makings of a stripper's locker.

Tiffany found the old man in his kitchen pouring two glasses of whiskey. He dropped a small white pill in 1, shook it up and then picked it up to give to Tiffany. She backed up before he could see her and went back into the bedroom to look continue looking around. The old man creeped up with drinks in hand.

"I figured you could use a drink," he suggested.

"Why thank you? I don't drink though," she sat the drink down hard on the television causing it to spill out on the tv.

"I thought all city women like to drink."

"Huge misconception."

"Oh, well why'd you really come back?" he asked unloosening his belt buckle.

"Not for your old man pee pee. That's for sure. Sir, I'm a police officer. You think I was going to let you get away with raping me?" asked Tiffany.

"Rape, I wouldn't never...and to an officer of the law. No way. You're going to consent," he asserted.

"Old dude you got it all wrong. I will kill you before I let you put your penis anywhere near me," said Tiffany drawing her weapon on the old man.

"You're going to shoot me?"

"No sir, not as long as you stay over there. I don't want to cause you any harm. I'm looking for my daughter. Now I'm going to leave out that door and you're going to stay right there until you hear my friend's truck leave this road. If you move, I will blow that old pisser right off and you will never have the opportunity of experiencing the heaven you like to call pussy again."

"I didn't mean to scare you but I thought you was coming on to me. I thought you gave me the eye."

"The eye! Negro please! You can barely see but you saw me giving you the eye? Is that why you put that pill in my drink?"

"You saw that? I was just trying to help. I read somewhere that older ladies like yourself sometimes have problems with wetness. I was trying to get your rivers flowing if you know what I mean," he explained.

"I just threw up in my mouth. Something is wrong with you! Who else you been giving those pills to? Your granddaughter? Is that why she doesn't come around so much?"

"Lady what type of filth are you implying! I would never touch my granddaughter. I might pay for a piece of pussy every now and again but I ain't no pedophile. Get the hell out my house," he screamed.

"I was leaving anyhow," said Tiffany backing up slowly keeping her pistol drawn on him as she exited his cabin swiftly. As she neared the door she caught a glimpse of a very new looking calendar with a scantily dressed girl on it. She snatched the calendar off the wall before leaving out. The girls featured in the calendar were featured strippers at the Candy Bar strip club in South Side Plaza.

Tiffany had stumbled onto her next clue and was out the door and in the passenger seat before the old man could come chasing behind her. Myshelle pulled off and sped down the road kicking up dirt and rocks all over the place.

"What happened in there?" asked Myshelle out of breath.

"Old bastard tried to rape me."

"What?"

"I caught him putting a roofie in a cup of whiskey he offered me. When I wouldn't drink it he decided he would get it anyway. I had to draw down on him but I did find our next clue on my way out. Check this out," said Tiffany handing Myshelle the calendar.

"What's this smut?" asked Myshelle holding the calendar with disgust.

"A promo calendar from the Candy Bar, either the old man is a customer or his granddaughter works there. And from the looks of what just happened I don't think he's seen any woman in person up close in years. "

"This is turning into a real circus of sorts."

"I'd say. Let me try Princess number again," said Tiffany dialing her number 2 speed dial. Her daughter's line continued to ring busy.

"I hope this chick is here so we can finally get some answers."

"Me too because I have no clue what move to make next."

"We'll figure it out together," said Myshelle hugging her friend.

The trip to the Candy Bar wasn't a total waste of time. They had managed to discover Shalonda's alias Mizz Phatnwet, and ode to her thickness and moisture level. Word on the street was that Mizz Phatnwet worked part time on Thursdays and Sundays only. She had no accurate contact information on file considering she was only 17 unbeknownst to them. They were able to find out that she kept a room at one of the motels on Midlothian Turnpike, a quintessential ho stroll of sorts.

"I'm starving," commented Myshelle as they drove in and out of the seedy motel parking lots looking for the infamous purple Honda Accord with Hello Kitty lashes.

"I don't even remember the last time I ate. I have no appetite."

"You've got to eat something. You'll make yourself sick."

"Too late. I've been sick. I'm running on fumes."

"Well there's a McDonald's up the street. We're grabbing something to eat when we leave out this lot," Myshelle said.

"Do you see that?" pointed Tiffany excitedly.

"What?"

"A purple Honda Civic with Hello Kitty lashes going pass us!"

"Oh shit, I'm on her," said Myshelle speeding up behind the little purple car.

The car sped through traffic weaving in and out almost losing Myshelle in the traffic. She stayed on her tail and followed her to the hotel behind Bob Evans. The car parked and a petite and shapely brown skin girl exits the car carrying a large green Michael Kors bag. They park a row behind her and follow her into the hotel. The young woman passes the front desk and heads straight to the elevator. She pushes the button and gets on when the doors open. Tiffany and Myshelle rush to see what floor she gets off on, the 2nd. They press the 2 in the elevator and get back on her trail. They catch her as she is swiping her key to Room 213. Just as the door almost shuts completely Tiffany pushed inside and forces the door open.

"Shalonda Eubanks?"

"Who are you?" the young woman screeched in fear.

"I'm Princess mother, Officer Saunders. Where is my daughter?"

"I don't know. I dropped her off at a guy's house. I swear."

"What guy's house? Justin?"

"No I picked her up from Justin's house. He was the decoy. She was going to see my friend Juice from round the way. I haven't talked to her since I dropped her off."

"What was she meeting Juice for?"

"I don't know. She liked him. She said something about needing protection."

"Oh my God, she's avoiding me because she was having sex with some boy!"

"I guess. I promise you I'm not lying. If you don't believe me, call him."

"You call him now," Tiffany demanded.

Shalonda or MizzPhatnwet dialed his number on her cell phone.

It rang once and someone picked up, "Juice".

"Juice this Phatnwet, that girl still with you?"

"Nah that bitch got put the fuck out."

"What bitch?" screamed Tiffany into the phone as she snatched it out of Shalonda's hand.

"Who da fuck is dis?" screamed Juice.

"Your worst fucking nightmare if you did anything to harm my daughter. Where are you Juice I'm coming for your ass right now?"

"Who's your daughter bitch?"

"Yo Juice calm down. This lady is a police officer. Where's Princess?" asked Shalonda.

"Fuck da police. Fuck dat Princess bish was dethroned. How about that?" he laughed.

"Where is this piece of shit at?" Tiffany screamed at Shalonda.

"The motel down the street," Shalonda divulged.

"Bitch you rattin' on me?" Juice yelled from the phone.

"Fuck you Juice," screamed Shalonda.

"Nah, fuck you bitch and that old hoe looking for her bitch ass daughter."

"Well I would assume that would be me and it'll never be fuck me young bra. You talk a good game over the phone. Save this old bitch from having to come look for you and just meet downstairs in like 5 minutes," propositioned Tiffany.

"HAAAAA, you funny. I ain't got shit to prove to your old ass. Like I said, fuck you and your daughter. That bitch won't down to suck dick so she got tossed just like I would do your ass but you old bitches nasty. I know you suck

dick," Juice laughed. His entourage in the background egged him on.

"Since you're going to force me to come looking for you, you're going to

wish you met me downstairs like I asked. It's all good though. See you

soon...Juice."

Tiffany hung up the phone in his face.

"Let's find this bitch nigga now," yelled Myshelle fired up.

"Let's go. You're going with us," said Tiffany pulling Shalonda by the arm

out the hotel room.

"What do you need from me?"

"Point out where this scum bag is and tell me who do you know that

works at the Grace Street precinct?"

"Juice could be at any of these hotels, we use them all at different times

for different reasons. It's hard to say."

"Well let's at least try. Don't sound like such a defeatist. Keep walking."

"Who do these knuckleheads think they are? Lord I swear, I want to slap

him, his momma for having him and his daddy for impregnating her. A whole slew of slapping going on," exclaimed Myshelle trying to control her mounting anxiety.

"A slap would be way too kind."

"You're right."

"What kind of car does this asshole Juice drive?"

"A white BMW. It has CNDYGL on the license plates," blurted Shalonda.

"Oh but you know his license plates though?"

"He's the connect."

"The connect to what?"

"To whatever. Pills, coke, dope, guns...girls. He can hook you up with whatever you need."

"I need my daughter," Tiffany stated firmly.

"I hope he can hook you up with that."

"You still haven't told me who's your friend at my precinct?"

"You already know I don't have any friends. That's obvious. You can't trust anybody out here in these streets. I survive on my own."

"You steal right?"

"Sometimes."

"You've been caught before. I'm certain of that. Your grandfather said he picks you up from the Grace Street precinct when you get in trouble. Who's looking out for you?"

"I'm looking out for myself. My granddad lied to you. He don't know what he talking about. You can't believe anything he says," pleaded Shalonda.

"I would love to say that I disagree but you're definitely right about not trusting anyone my baby is still missing so it is what it is. Now let's go find Juice," insisted Tiffany.

Things continued to work in the determined mother's favor as they patrolled the parking lots of the seedy motels searching for a needle in a haystack. Three motels down and several left to go when they spotted a pretty shiny nice white BMW parked with CNDYGL on the license plates.

"Good work Shalonda. What room is he staying in?"

"I don't know. He switch up all the time. Just please let me go since I helped you track him down. Now you can do whatever you want to and I can go on about my business."

"I don't think so. Our business will be done when my daughter turns up, till then you're my property," explained Tiffany to Myshelle, "don't let Mizz Thing go, she's rolling with us. Keep your foot on the gas pedal just in case."

"Word life son," nodded Myshelle in agreement.

"You still got Ty's bat from softball in here?"

"Yeah it's in the trunk but what you going to do with that that you can't use your gun for?"

"Unlock the doors for me please," said Tiffany returning her weapon to its holster on her hip. She withdrew the baseball bat from the trunk and walked over slowly to the beautiful BMW eyeing it from hood to trunk. She was going to hate doing what she was about to because she loved herself some BMW's.

"What is she going to do with that bat?" asked Shalonda scared.

"Just watch," smirked Myshelle.

Tiffany outstretched her arms to yawn and knocked out the driver's side head light. She then began to work herself around the vehicle taking shots at it with the baseball bat. Next she tried to hit a home run through his windshield sending tinted shards of glass shattered everywhere. Just as she was about to make some minor adjustments to the fender, an enraged and angry man boy

155

erupts from inside the hotel room spilling down the staircase with his pistol in his hand.

"Bitch what the fuck? I could kill you," screamed the man presumed to be Juice.

Tiffany set the baseball bat down on the trunk of the car making sure to cause another small dent. As he approached her with all his rage, she walked toward him and cocked her two fingers back like a pistol before holding it right to his forehead.

"I would really try to get control of your emotions," Tiffany suggested demurely.

"You the bitch from the phone?" Juice barked.

"No, I'm the Police Officer from the phone," she said displaying her badge.

"Whoa, what the fuck! You can't do this to my car, who do you think you are?"

"Oh the police officer in me didn't vandalize and damage your car. That was purely the bitch in me that time."

"So you think you protected because you got a badge bitch?"

"No young man, let me ask you the questions! Do you think you're protected because I have a badge? Young man who won't live to be old man?" Tiffany said toying with him.

"What?"

"Exactly. I'm here on official business. My daughter Princess was last seen with you. You think your car look bad wait till I'm done with you…but we're going to get to the bottom of where my daughter is," explained Tiffany drawing her service pistol on him.

"Shalonda why you bring this bitch here?"

Before Shalonda could respond Tiffany smacked the young thug in his face with the gun knocking blood out his mouth.

"What the…you're going to lose your fucking badge when I'm done with you!"

"Fuck this badge and this job. You can have it! I want my daughter back. And I want her back now," screamed Tiffany.

"Okay, let me get my shit together. Lady, your daughter was here briefly. No disrespect...okay maybe it's too late for that. My fault. But I haven't seen your daughter since she walked out here on her own. I swear to you on my kids' life," Juice proclaimed.

"How many kids you have Juice?"

"7 and I take care every one of em'."

"Good. What would you do if one of your baby mommas called you and said one of your kids was missing?"

"I'd be tearing this fuggin' city apart looking for em," he confessed.

"You sound like a good dude but make no mistake, I find myself in that exact situation right now. My daughter needs help. I know she does. So you understand why I stand here with my gun in your face looking for answers?"

Juice tried not to look Tiffany in the eyes. She got him. He was emotionally on the line. In an instant his whole disposition changed.

"I understand. I don't like what you did to my car but I respect the fuck outta that shit because I see the hurt in your eyes. Ma'am, I'm sorry I don't know more. I'm sorrier I even came off at you like that over the phone," he said more tempered.

"I appreciate that but it's a lot more destruction and possibly death that lies ahead for this city if my daughter doesn't turn up soon."

"Hey, do what you gotta do. But please please please, and I say again please...miss me with that please. I promise if there is anything I can do to help you find your daughter I will do it."

"I appreciate your cooperation, really I do. So I'm going to remove my weapon from your face," she said putting her pistol back in its holster.

"Thank you. Tell me what you need me to do, and I'm on it," begged Juice.

"I need answers Juice. When my daughter left here something happened to her...she didn't come back home. I need you to make some calls, find out what you can and get back with me quickly. Time is of the essence and every second I can't locate her I know she's in danger."

"It's nuffin' what's your number?"

Tiffany pulled her card out and handed it to him.

"I'm sorry about your car," Tiffany offered genuinely.

"It's nuffin' Ma, I got excellent car insurance. I'm going to do anything I can to help you. My moms' is dead but I know if she was here and she could do something to help me, I know she would break her back to. I respect you and why you doing it. I'll be calling you soon."

"Nuff said Juice. Thanks," Tiffany mocked.

CHAPTER VII:

TROUBLE LURKS

Tiffany woke up on her couch in a daze. The prior day events were a blur and she was hoping to wake up from the nightmare she felt like she was trapped in. She ran to Princess bedroom to see if she had been dreaming all along. No such luck, her daughter was still missing. Tiffany checked her cellphone for missed calls. None. Text messages. None.

"Damn," screamed out Tiffany in horror.

"What's wrong?" Myshelle ran in the bedroom shouting as if an intruder had broken in.

"My baby, I miss her so much. I pray to God she's okay," she broke down in tears.

"I know. She's okay Tiff. We're going to find her," consoled Myshelle as best she could.

"They haven't even released the Amber Alert yet. My baby could be halfway across the world by now. You know I see this shit all day every day. I never thought this would happen to my own daughter."

"I know," cried Myshelle holding Tiffany.

"Is Shalonda sleep?"

"Of course. That child ate and passed out on the floor. I don't know when the last time she had some real rest. She went straight to sleep."

"Good. Hopefully when she wakes up she'll be in a better mood to tell us who's looking out for her at my precinct."

"And if not?"

"I don't know. I gotta make a move. Princess life is dependent on it."

"Well whatever you want to do, I got your back."

"Thanks. I'm not going to lie; I thank God for you right now. I don't know how I would be able to deal if you weren't here. Thank you."

"You don't have to thank me. Dionne said it best...that's what friends are for," said Myshelle trying to force a smile through her sadness.

"Good ol' Dionne Warwick," remarked Tiffany wanting to be in better mood but lacking the emotional and mental motivation needed to do so.

"Listen, I know this is a lot for you. I can't even begin to comprehend what you're feeling. Just know that you aren't alone. I know things are truly messed up in my own life but we have your back. That's my Goddaughter. That's Rod's Goddaughter. You know we can make a few calls. Rod will put that work in himself."

"I know and I'm glad that if I need to make that call. I will. In the meantime, I'm going to handle this work myself. I can't drag you or Rod into this too much. The fact is my baby could be dead, she could be held against her will. I have no clue and I work in the police department. I know how these cases end. I have hope, a little faith and am praying that Princess is alive and well...but I'm preparing myself for the worst Myshelle. If my baby doesn't turn up alive or dead in maybe 1 or 2 more days, I'm not certain how much more I can endure personally," she sobbed.

"Real talk Tiff, my kids are damn near grown. We'll be sharing a cell in jail if necessary," asserted Myshelle.

"I know you mean that too but I'm probably going to hell for what I'll do for my daughter."

"Whew, now that's deep. I was with you till you went there; you know I love me some Jesus. I can't fool with you on that but everything else that don't include being damned to hell, I'm down for," she joked.

"So adultery yes? Murder...no?" joked Tiffany too soon.

Myshelle's face saddened, "I just want you to know that I'm not saying I got your back because it sounds good. Or because I feel like I owe that to you for what I did…no, you're my sister. Not only did we grow up together but we raised all our kids together as a family. And that's what families do. They stick together no matter what. Whatever has to happen to get our girl back, let's just make a move."

"You're dead serious," smiled Tiffany.

"Dead ass," shrugged Myshelle.

"My rider," said Tiffany giving Myshelle dap that turned into a hug.

"Always sis," she said hugging her back.

"Okay let's get off this mushy shit though. I hate crying. I'm already way too emotional. I need you to do me a favor first though."

"Anything," agreed Myshelle.

"Please go talk to your husband before we do anything."

"What?"

"You just basically agreed to go on a murderous killing spree with me if you have to. Don't you think you should discuss that with your husband? I know he's angry with you for the affair with Chris but he loves you. God forbid something should happen to us."

"He doesn't want to talk to me. Plus, he might shoot me on site. I don't want to be in the paper for that story...husband shoots wife after steamy affair."

"If he shoots you, I'll shoot him. New story...betrayed friend shoots husband of cheating best friend," laughed Tiffany.

"That's a fucked up story. Oh my gosh, just cover me while I go in. If I'm not out in 16 minutes call for back up."

"Why 16 minutes?"

"If he accepts my apology and we end up making love on the kitchen floor."

"Gotcha."

"I'm just saying. You just said we might die doing this shit. I want my last piece to be with my husband."

"Aww, that's sweet. I think. Go handle your biz. I'm going to call the precinct and Will. Good luck."

"Thanks," she said reluctantly walking to her house next door that she hadn't been inside in days. Myshelle was so nervous turning her key in the lock. She almost expected a hidden bomb to detonate and blow her to smithereens. There might as well been that scary horror music playing in the background the way she felt walking inside the house she had called home for so long. The kids should have been gone doing one of their many activities. She saw his truck parked outside so she assumed he was home. As she crept through quietly her next fear became whether there was another woman inside her home. Tiffany was going to be pissed if she got them locked up before they could even look for Princess. She prayed it wasn't the latter and continued to look for her husband.

When she rounded the corner into the den she ran straight into him walking in from the garage.

"Sorry I was just looking for you," she said nervously backing away from TyRod.

"What are you doing here?" he asked almost business like.

"I mean I do live here...still."

"I thought that too but I can't remember the last night you slept here. I was wondering when the change of address was going to pop up. I thought you and your mother were roommates now."

"Rod you didn't want me here."

"Damn right and I still don't. Which brings me back to my original question? What are you doing here?" he repeated after clearing his throat.

"I didn't even want to do this. This was Tiffany's idea."

"Well bye. When did you start taking orders from Tiffany? I can't even believe she's talking to you."

"Well for the record, neither can I but clearly you've been in your own world. Princess is missing. She hasn't been seen in over 24 hours. There's supposed to be an Amber Alert but it hasn't been released. Tiffany's afraid something really fucked up happened to her. I just came to tell you I might get locked up when it's all said and done."

"What have you done?"

"Nothing...yet. Not that much...yet."

"And who are you two supposed to be some black Laverne and Shirley?"

"No wise guy! What would you do if something happened to one of our kids?"

"You right. I understand for her but why are you taking that ride with her?"

"Because she would do the same for us."

"What about Will? Princess has a father."

"Rod are you for real? You talking about the Pastor seriously."

"He may have had a hard life before he found God. If anybody should be ready to take that ride or die role, it needs to be Princess dad. Not you. I can't have my wife out here playing around in these streets. Tiffany is a police officer. She can play around with the law. That's what cops do anyway. You on the other hand are a wife and a mother. You're going to get yourself hurt. What about our kids? Who's going to raise them if you get locked up?"

"Raise them. Where are they now? Our kids are almost grown. They really don't need me for much these days. Yet still I love them and I'm going to be there for them always. I just need you to not agree with what I'm doing but don't try to stop me."

"Well let me go too."

"You stay here. If we need you, we can call you. Somebody has to stay free to tell our story," smiled Myshelle.

"Yeah free is good on me. I don't want to go to jail. I love Princess a lot but I want to stay on the right side of the law. You ladies got that whole "Orange is the New Black" thing going on. Y'all could make that work but I would miss the hell out of you."

"I'm sorry for what I did. I truly am. I love you with everything in my being but I've been needing more from you and feeling like I'm running into a brick wall. I pray you can one day forgive me for the trespasses I've made against our marriage."

"Forgiveness is the easy part, trying to forget what you did is the hardest part. I keep seeing that shit in my mind, playing over and over again. I have no right to judge or be angry with you considering my past mistakes but I'm just very hurt."

"I know. If God give me the chance to fix this with you after this, I want to."

"We already have, just make sure you come back in one piece. If shit gets thick, I need you to call me. You still my wife first. I know Tiffany is a gung ho lady cop, you're my wife. If anybody look like they a problem, call me. You promise me that?"

"Of course I can," she said wrapping her arms around her husband's waist as she pulled him towards her to kiss him.

TyRod kissed her back while running his hands down her backside. Rod couldn't deny his love for his wife. He was beyond mad that she had betrayed him and yet so close to home. He knew he didn't have time to judge, point fingers or berate. He didn't expect his wife to get into any real trouble that Tiffany wouldn't be able to get them out of but he knew things were going rampant in the world. Even if you weren't looking for trouble it somehow landed in your lap. Certainly Princess being missing meant trouble and would only bring about more trouble for all involved. So he gave his approval and made love to his wife as if it could be the last time he got to touch her.

"I need my phone," cried out Myshelle from the kitchen floor. She jumped up from the floor half naked to retrieve her phone. She sent a three-word message to Tiffany: need more time.

"What's wrong" asked TyRod looking confused from the floor.

"Nothing, I just text Tiffany. She was supposed to come in guns blazing if I wasn't out in 16 minutes."

"Oh okay," he said nonchalantly.

Myshelle sent the message, put her phone down and straddled her husband who awaited her on the kitchen floor. It was more than her body that called for him and his erectness. Her soul longed for the only man she ever loved. They were like two puzzle pieces connected for a bigger picture. It didn't matter what was wrong with their relationship or their lives at that moment. He needed her. She needed him. The sex was the icing on the cake, they both were looking for that reconnection to each other. When they just needed each other. Their lovemaking was slow and deliberate. Time stood still. Myshelle got lost laying in her husband's embrace. It had been such a long time since they just laid together and felt each other's warmness and enjoyed being in the other's presence.

Myshelle woke to the sound of her cell phone vibrating on the floor. She picked it up. It was a message from Tiffany: I'll be back. Got a lead.

"Shit, I gotta go babe. Tiff might have found something," she said as she scrambled to get dressed.

"What?" he yelled startled by his wife's sudden departure.

"Tiffany just text me. She went somewhere. She says she might have a lead. I got to catch up with her."

"Honey just wait here till she comes back. You don't even know where she's going?"

"I'm texting her now," she fumbled with her phone nervously.

TyRod saw the fear and anxiety in her eyes. He jumped up and held his wife tight, "calm down. Tiffany will be okay. Just wait till she gets back. I don't want you running around here by yourself. It's one thing when you two were going to be together but it's not safe."

"Rod you know I'm strapped."

He laughs, "I know. That's why I definitely think you need to wait here for Tiff to get back. If she responds to your message and tell you where to meet her, you can go. If not, I don't think so."

"But Baby."

"I know. She'll be back. Tiff is good. You know she can hold her own."

"I know that but she should have somebody there with her. What if she finds her baby dead or something Rod? She shouldn't be alone doing this."

"Princess is going to be okay. I don't think for one second somebody killed her. I pray not. Go," he blurted out.

"Thanks babe, I love you. I'll be back. I promise," Myshelle said running out the back door to Tiffany's house next door. She opened the door and looked inside the den, Shalonda was gone with Tiffany. She checked her phone for a response back from Tiffany. Nothing. Without knowing where Tiffany went she was stuck. She dialed her number and hoped she answer.

"Hello," said Tiffany from the other end of the phone.

"Where you going?"

"Juice called me. He told me that a week ago some Russian guys showed up around the way looking for a drug connect and girls. Really more girls than drugs. Since these guys have showed up at least 3 other young black girls Princess age have also gone missing. I found out the missing persons reports have all traced back to my precinct."

"What," mouthed Myshelle in disbelief.

"So where are you on your way to now?"

"Looking for the Russians."

"Where though?"

"He said they like to drink and kick it with the ladies."

"Candy Bar?"

"Yep."

"I'll meet you there." Myshelle ended the call and put her phone in the passenger seat next to her. She pushed the gas pedal hard, she didn't want Tiffany to make a move without her. Surprisingly Myshelle avoided a speeding ticket as she violated speed limits all across the city. When she pulled into the parking lot she scanned the lot for Tiffany's beat up Camry. She was parked all the way in the back of the lot, closer to Shopper's World. Myshelle parked two rows down and jumped out to get in the car with Tiffany. Shalonda was sitting in the front seat, so she hopped in the back seat.

"Hey what I miss?" asked Myshelle.

"So much...for starters guess who knows our Russian friends we are looking for?"

Myshelle pointed at Shalonda.

"Yes, she's danced for them twice. Apparently they are good tippers that wanted some top. She claims she was too scared so she sent them another way."

"Why didn't you tell us about the Russians before?" asked Myshelle aggravated.

"Because you didn't ask about the Russians! Y'all asked about Princess," exclaimed Shalonda.

"Yeah but you knew these Russians liked young girls. That information would have been helpful much sooner. Don't ya think?"

"I'm sorry. This is a lot for me right now. I'm trying to help. I don't have to be here," she pouted and grabbed the door handle to leave.

"And where do you think you're going? You were the last person I can guarantee saw my daughter, you and I are bosom buddies until she turns up. Now you can play along, be helpful and take this ride or I'll take your ass down to lockup. I'll charge you with so much shit you won't be able to get a bond."

"I told you everything I know. I don't know where these Russian guys stay because I did not go with them that night. I didn't trust them. They look like the type to rape you and then shoot you in the head."

"Who did you send them to?"

"My frenemy Becky. She a crazy ass white girl that will do anything for a dollar including getting raped and shot in the head. Stupid bitch."

"Is Becky at work now?"

"She might be."

"I need you to go get her and bring her out here. I don't want to go inside because the Russians may be inside now. Go in, check the scene out, see if you see our guys, if not find Becky or get a contact number for her. We need to talk to her."

"Okay, after this can I go?" asked Shalonda frustrated.

"You can go when I find Princess. Now go inside and hurry up," Tiffany demanded.

Shalonda shrugged as she followed the orders.

"The nerve of this heifer," said Myshelle in disgust.

"I'm going to end up shooting this chick. I can feel it," Tiffany sighed. She yawned and tried to fight the worry, stress and fatigue that had long ago set in.

"This is totally crazy. Russians?"

"That's what I said", Tiffany pauses, "you and Rod good now?"

Myshelle looked at her slyly, "what makes you think?"

"Need more time," she giggled.

They both burst out laughing together for a second.

"Yes, we're good. Thank you very much."

"Good. I'm glad. At least something is going right. Maybe this is a sign that we'll find Princess."

"We're going to find her."

"I pray so."

Shalonda scurried back into the car nervously, "okay, Becky was there but she didn't want to come outside. She doesn't like talking to the police. She did write down where the Russians are staying."

"I oughta go in there and drag her out here. She doesn't like talking to police? You young kids these days!"

"No, I don't think she meant any disrespect. I think one of her parents were killed by the police. She's just traumatized. She assured me this address is legit. I told her you were going to come back for her if she gave you some bullshit. Here," said Shalonda handing Tiffany the napkin.

"Thanks you," said Tiffany looking at the address.

"Where is that?" asked Myshelle.

"Near River Road."

"It's nice out there."

"That's where we are on our way to right now. Let's switch cars though. We're going to look suspicious as hell riding in that neighborhood in this car. Now if I had a pizza sign on top, we'd be good."

The three temporarily abandoned the beat up car for the luxury SUV.

"You drive," said Myshelle tossing Tiffany the keys.

Shalonda went to get in the front seat of the beautiful cayenne Range Rover TyRod had gifted his wife when Myshelle grabbed her by her arm and stopped her before she could even sit down good, "Girl bye! Get in the back seat. This is my ride! Thank you," she said sitting in the passenger seat and slamming the door in the young teens face. Shalonda adjusted her face from disgust to a fraudulent and phony half smile before climbing in the back seat.

"That's why I didn't like these cars. These backseats are way too small for fucking. I wouldn't have bought this," Shalonda taunted.

"Little girl you have a purple Honda accord with Hello Kitty lashes. I don't have to laugh out loud because I'm laughing silently on the inside," spat Myshelle.

"You just mad."

"Mad cause what. That we're stuck with your ignorant ass until we find my God daughter? Yes. Proceed with caution little girl."

"Duly noted old lady," barked back Shalonda.

"Hey, chill out before I put your ass in handcuffs. You're here on official business only. For the record I wouldn't mess with her, she got a helluva' windmill slap," suggested Tiffany to Shalonda.

"You won't even see it coming till Boom...you just got slapped in the face," confirmed Myshelle.

"Let's just make the next move. Puh-lease, y'all in the way of my business right now."

"Baby girl, you have no business until my daughter is found. Understood?"

"Understood," agreed Shalonda.

"Did she give you their names?"

"Yes. The dark haired one is Artyom. He goes by Art. The other is the blonde dude, his name is Vadim."

"Good job," complimented Tiffany as she drove to the address on Westham Parkway, a street in one of the nicer neighborhood in the area. When Tiffany turned on the block, she passed the house in question as it sat on the corner. She went down the block and made a U-turn before parking in front of one of the houses on the block a few doors down.

"So what now?" asked Shalonda curiously.

"We wait. We watch. We need to see what's going on here or find out where else they go."

"Wake me up when we're leaving," requested Shalonda.

"This is so exciting and scary at the same time," commented Myshelle.

"First stakeout huh?" asked Tiffany already full aware of the answer.

"Yes. We should have gotten some coffee and doughnuts."

"That would have been a good idea," interrupted Shalonda from the backseat.

"I thought you were going to sleep?" Myshelle asked.

"I'm hungry. Sue me."

"We'll get food in a little while. For now, we sit and wait," Tiffany reiterated.

Hours went by before there was any movement or sign of life inside the house. Shortly after the sun set a black Ford F350 pulled into the driveway and two large white guys climbed out the truck. One was blonde, the other was dark haired, presumably Art and Vadim. They looked around their surroundings hesitantly almost as if they knew someone was watching them. Tiffany and Myshelle crouched down in their seats as to not be seen. The two men enter the house through the front door and close it behind them. Instantly lights came on within the house and it almost seemed to come alive.

"I've got to get a closer look," said Tiffany opening the car door and sprinting closer to the house. She got close enough to the perimeter to see inside the back windows. There were girls, young girls in the house. Tiffany ran back to the car anxious and excited at the same time.

"There are girls in that house," Tiffany proclaimed.

"Stop playing! You think Prin is inside?"

"I think there's a good chance she's in there."

"How do we get inside though?" asked Myshelle.

"I don't know but we need to think of something quick."

"I have an idea," she screeched.

"I'm almost afraid to ask."

"It's genius. Pure genius."

CHAPTER VIII:

MOMMA'S GOT A PLAN

"I don't think this is going to work. You're going to get us killed," complained Shalonda.

"Did we ask you for your opinion?" Myshelle blurted.

"I'm just saying."

"It's our best shot. I don't see either of you coming up with a better plan," barked Tiffany.

"I think I should sit this part out," weaseled Myshelle.

If I could do this on my own, I would but the fact is that I need you two. If you won't do this for me do it for Princess."

"I could sure use a drink right about now," Myshelle said looking down at her clothing or lack thereof. Normally she wouldn't dare wear such risqué attire outside of the house but she would do anything for her kids, Princess included. It didn't hurt that she looked cute in a black body dress with slashes and slits all over it exposing her brown flesh underneath. She wore black thigh high stockings and clear stiletto pumps. Myshelle certainly looked the part, now she just had to play the part and convince these possible Russian assailants that she was a stripper/masseuse.

Standing next to Tiffany who looked more like a video vixen than a distraught mother in search of her daughter, Myshelle regained her courage. "You look so authentic," laughed Myshelle trying to break the tension up.

"What?" asked Tiffany.

"That was supposed to be a compliment."

Tiffany couldn't help but not be amused with Myshelle's distraction mechanisms or coping techniques. She looked at her best friend sternly with a gaze so sharp it could kill from miles away.

"I'm sorry. I'm just very nervous again," Myshelle explained.

"You've never stripped before?" asked Shalonda in disbelief.

"Only for my husband Shalonda!"

"Well just pretend you're dancing for him. Block out the faces or close your eyes. Either one always works for me."

"You mean you have to close your eyes to get through it?"

"Not all the time. Some nights are tougher, I can't speak for nobody but me. Sometimes I want the stares to stop. Or at least what they are looking at...see something different," Shalonda remarked.

"Stop stripping then. That's easy."

"Easy for who. How else am I supposed to make a living? At least I'm not prostituting on the street."

"But you do it in the club. If you dance for dollars, you're doing Lord knows what else for it too. That's not passing judgment on you, that's just feeling bad for you. Life is hard enough out here. You putting yourself in situations like these isn't going to make it easier for you," said Myshelle.

"It's not like that though. I don't do it all the time but sometimes I just do what I have to. Y'all met my grandfather, it's no way I can live with him on a day to day basis... but he's all the family I've got. Ain't that fucked up? Abusive old horny fuck left to care for a little girl," Shalonda laughed through the tears.

"Why do you go back?" asked Tiffany wiping the young girl's tears away.

"I get scared out here. I've been beaten and raped so many times. Sometimes I just want to get away from it all. My grandfather's house is the safest place I know. He's quicker than the rest," she sniffled.

"I'm sorry. I wish I didn't have to ask you to do this with me now."

"It's cool. For the first time it will be for something and somebody other than myself. Princess doesn't need this life I'm living."

"When this is over I want you to stay with me. You don't ever have to go back to your grandfather's house again or anywhere that is truly unsafe for you. If you don't want to stay with me I can help you get placed somewhere, just don't turn back now. You don't look like you like this lifestyle."

"I don't but we're not all blessed to come from good situations, you know?"

"I do know but that doesn't determine the quality of life you create for yourself. I don't have the best family situation, my mother raised me alone. Never mentioned my father to me a day in my life as if this man never existed. Like she magically impregnated herself, "chuckled Myshelle.

"My father raised me because my mother was crazy before it was considered hip. She spent a lot of time in and out of hospitals. We all have our own shit, and that's not to take away from anything you've suffered or endured at the hands of your grandfather or anyone else. I just need you to be stronger than the pain you feel. You are so young with so much life ahead of you," said Tiffany.

"She's right. We'll help you anyway we can. Just give yourself a chance to see what else life has to offer," Myshelle added.

"Princess is lucky to have you two in her life," sobbed Shalonda.

"And now you have us too. Truly, we can do this without you. If you are stepping away from this life, I want you to do so completely. You can wait in the car. Myshelle and I should be able to handle this," Tiffany said matter of factly.

"We can?" asked Myshelle in disbelief.

"Yes we can, and we will."

"No I want to do this. This will be my last dance. I want to help."

"Cool. Well then ladies let's stick to the plan. Any questions?"

"No, it's pretty simple and straight forward. We go in and dance, you excuse yourself to the bathroom so you can check for Princess. Either way we're in and out in 30 minutes' tops," recounted Shalonda.

"Exactly."

"Let's go before I lose my nerve," sighed Myshelle.

The ladies strutted their respective stuff's across the cement pavers walkway that separated the beautiful lush green lawn to the front door of the house the Russians were occupying. Tiffany knocked hard three times in a row.

"Who is it?" said the thick Russian accent from behind the door.

"I'm Twizler from the Candy Bar. You are receiving complimentary dances and massages for 2 VIP," laid on Tiffany.

"We didn't order this."

"Yes, I know. This private session is compliments of management for your business."

"Who are your friends?"

"MizzPhatnwet and Lady Puss."

"Hold on," said the voice.

Tiffany looked at the keyhole hoping they would open the door and allow them in. The longer it took for the Russian to come back to the door, the more nervous Tiffany became. What if they called the Candy Bar to confirm the gift? Tiffany hoped they were not that thorough. Just as Tiffany was about to leave the door swung open. One of the two Russians stood there and welcomed the dance trio inside.

"How nice of the club? Who should we thank?"

"The manager."

"Okay, come in ladies. Make yourself's comfortable."

"Thank you," they said in unison.

"So what exactly do we get for free?" he asked eagerly closing the door behind them.

"A 30-minute dance and massage."

"No fuck?" he asked curiously.

"Oh I'm sorry that's up to the girls personally. So if you're nice enough, you never know..."

"Where do you want to set up?"

"A bedroom. That way I can have you lie down flat on your stomach."

"Ahh, yes, very nice. Do we both go at the same time, or one at a time. How?" he questioned readily.

"We do the dance first then the massages last, separately."

"No dance just massages."

"The session is designed to include the dance. While the two ladies dance I set up the massages in the separate rooms. It's really very standard," confirmed Tiffany.

"We'll see about that," he replied.

"My girls and I need to get ready, is there a bathroom?" asked Tiffany while surveying the house.

"Follow me," he said leading them to a bathroom off the main hallway. They passed by several sparsely furnished rooms en route to the bathroom. He opened the bathroom door for them and watched them file in one after the other.

"Thanks, give us a few minutes to freshen up," advised Tiffany closing the door behind them.

"That was too easy," whispered Myshelle nervously.

"I'd say but let's just get this done and get out. Remember stick to the plan, don't stop dancing. Keep them focused on the dance till I finish looking around," she whispered back.

"Okay," they agreed in unison.

Tiffany opened the bathroom door and followed her counterparts to the main room where both Russians were now seated eagerly.

"Ladies, this is Vadim and I'm Art," said the biggest one jumping to his feet.

"Nice to meet you Art, you already know I'm Twizler, these are my girls MizzPhatnwet and Lady Puss," she said allowing her hand to be kissed by Art.

"You all are very beautiful. Would you like a drink?" he asked pointing to the beverage cart to the right of the sofa.

"Of course but I'll serve. You gentlemen relax, we are here to serve you." Tiffany walked over to the cart and picked up 5 short ball glasses and filled them all up halfway with the first dark liquor she grabbed. As she dropped a cube of ice into each glass, she sneezed into her hand and knocked some ice on the carpet. As she bent down to pick it up she removed 4 small white pills she hid in her bra. She put two in one glass and two in another and watched them dissolve before topping it off with a little more alcohol. Once she was certain the pill was undetectable at first glance she picked up the two spiked drinks and handed one to each man. They took 2 large gulps and were finished both drinks in a matter of seconds. That made Tiffany and the other women feel better. They already knew what Tiffany had done and were just waiting till the pills kicked in. Tiffany then handed her partners in crime their respective drinks before she began sipping hers.

"Now let's get down to business. Art will you show me the rooms you gentlemen want to be massaged in. I have some ambience I want to add to the atmosphere while you watch your private show."

"Sure...that sounds really nice," he beamed.

Tiffany followed Art and his broad shoulders and back upstairs to the second floor. There were several rooms all with closed presumed locked doors. He showed her to the two closest rooms and gave her permission to set up in each room.

"Thanks, this is nice."

"Don't touch the other doors," he ordered.

"Yesss! These two rooms will be great. Now get back downstairs before you miss the best part of the show," she teased.

"We could start our own show right now," he suggested.

"We could when we're done. Business is business though. My boss will lose it if he finds out we didn't follow protocol. You know these guys, sticklers for routines," she laughed playfully as she touched his shoulder suggestively.

"I understand. I'll get out your way...for now." Tiffany signed with relief as he left her alone. She waited until she could no longer hear footsteps on the stairs and then proceeded to leave the room to look around. All of the upstairs rooms were locked with the exception of the bathroom door. Most of the house appeared to be unlived in. The bathroom was closer to filthy than nice. It looked like the bathroom of a girl's dorm room. There were tampon and panty liner wrappers piled up in the trash can. The less than attractive ring around the tub looked weeks if not months old. Where there were feminine hygiene products surely there were females thought Tiffany. She ran back into the bedrooms and set up tea light candles and oils on the dresser in each room.

She then crept downstairs to the kitchen. There were loaves of bread, sandwich meat and diet sodas stocked in the refrigerator. She found keys on a hanging wall organizer and begin looking through them for the one that fit the door that led to the garage. After trying 6 different keys she found the one that unlocked the door and allowed her to enter the garage. Inside there was a white cargo van and clothes racks that held hundreds of sexy outfits in all colors and styles. There was also a trash can on a work counter filled with cell phones of all makes and models. A noise from the inside startled Tiffany and sent her back inside to check on Myshelle and Shalonda.

When Tiffany walked back in the living room Shalonda had apparently morphed into MizzPhatnwet one last time because she was shaking and twerking her assets in front of the happy audience. Myshelle stood off to the side trying to bring herself to do what she was supposed to be doing. Lucky for them it didn't matter, because both of their eyes were glued to Shalonda. Tiffany concluded that they were okay before she took the keys that she found upstairs to the locked bedrooms. She fumbled through the keys trying to not to make any noise when she unlocked the first door. She burst inside almost expecting to see hordes of girls smuggled inside. The room was empty. She raced to check the other rooms. They were all empty too. But why keep empty rooms locked thought Tiffany? There had to be girls somewhere, she had seen them from the window. She looked all over the upstairs miffed at where they could have been hiding these girls.

As Tiffany looked up to the heavens for some sort of sign, she realized that there was an attic or crawl space above them. She would need help trying to get into the crawl space with no ability to move furniture or cause too much of a noise. She decided to go get Myshelle to help her. Back downstairs Shalonda was now straddled on the lap of Vadim grinding on him as he sat back fixated in delight.

"My bra is stuck; I'm going to borrow Lady Puss to help me unhinge it. Be right back," she said pulling Myshelle upstairs.

"Did you find anything?"

"Not yet. It's signs all over the house. I think there's an attic above us but I need help reaching the pulldown stairs from the ceiling."

"Don't you think they are going to hear us?" asked Myshelle worried.

"Maybe but I'm hoping those pills will be kicking in soon."

"It feels like we been here forever. We've got to hurry up. We can't leave her down there alone."

"She can handle these guys besides we aren't going to let anything happen to her. Let's just hurry up. We're both going to stand on this dresser

195

where I'll give you a boost to the ceiling. Grab the cord and pull the stairs down slowly."

They took their shoes off quietly and sat them down on the floor. Myshelle watched Tiffany climb atop the dresser and she followed suit. Both standing on the dresser Myshelle clasped her hands together for Myshelle to step in. She lifted her friend with all of her power until she was able to grasp the cord barely between her two fingers. Myshelle held onto the cord as Tiffany let her down slowly on the dresser. The stairs had been redone because they came down smoothly and quietly which was totally unexpected. Tiffany jumped off the dresser and slowly climbed the stairs. As she peered inside the dark attic from the pullout steps she began to make out the whites of eyes looking back at her. At a first glance there were at least 10 girls all ages, sizes and races surrounding the stairs.

Tiffany gasped in horror and delight, "sshh I'm here to help but I need you all to stay quiet a little longer."

The girls nodded in agreement as Tiffany backed up down the stairs.

"Nothing huh?" asked Myshelle.

Tiffany shook her head in disagreement. She held up 10 fingers.

"Girls. Lots of them. We gotta get them out of here."

"Princess?" she almost screeched.

"I can't see clearly. Maybe. Let's go back downstairs," she ordered.

As Tiffany and Myshelle turned around to go back downstairs Shalonda was coming upstairs.

"I was looking for you two. The Russians are out cold," giggled Shalonda.

"Good, that's perfect timing. There are girls hidden upstairs in the attic."

"Princess?"

"Not sure yet but let's get them out of here now before our Russian pals come to," said Tiffany running back up the attic stairs, "ladies, let's go quietly. One at a time come down and go outside and sit on the curb, I'm a police officer here to help."

The young women shrieked in delight. They had finally been saved. One by one each girl exited the attic and followed Tiffany's instructions. With each girl that exited the attic Tiffany hoped that one would be her daughter. Eventually there were 14 girls released from the attic and captivity against their will. Tiffany then called her captain to inform him of her findings and to request backup. Before the police arrived Tiffany had Myshelle and Shalonda hide in Myshelle's truck. Tiffany still had no clue who Shalonda's contact at her precinct was and she didn't want to give anyone clue as to who was helping her.

Within two hours there was a media frenzy outside of the home. Word had gotten out that 14 victims of sex trafficking had been discovered and efforts were being made to reconnect the young women with their families all over the world. Tiffany was glad to help the girls out but she was still no closer to finding her own daughter. Tiffany was being called a hero. It's just too bad she didn't feel like one. As she prepared to leave the scene her ex-partner Jeff found her as she started walking toward Myshelle's truck parked near the crime scene.

"Hey I've been looking for you," he remarked out of breath.

"I was just about to leave. This is kind of bitter sweet you know?"

"I know but we are going to find her. Do you mind my asking what you're doing out here? This was great but you could have gotten yourself hurt. You shouldn't be doing this type of vigilante stuff alone; you work for the police force."

"Is that what you think this is? My baby is still God knows where. I'm fucking desperate. I don't want to lose my daughter."

"You're not going to lose her."

"How can you be so sure? Do you even know how long some of those girls had been held against their will? When was the last time most of them seen their mother's faces? Months and years Jeff and you want me to wait on the police department."

"I know you're emotionally invested in this but you've got to let us do our job."

"Which is? What leads do you have?"

"Not many but we are working."

"And so am I."

"Tiffany let's not bump heads on this. Let me help you."

"I've given you and the department ample time to help me. It's about damn time I help myself. Good night Jeff," said Tiffany climbing into Myshelle's truck and pulling off in a hurry.

When Tiffany got around the corner Shalonda and Myshelle sat upright in their seats.

"Was that Jeff's voice I heard?" asked Shalonda.

"How do you know Jeff?" asked Tiffany stunned.

"That's my contact at the precinct. I've known him for years."

"In what capacity? That's my old partner."

"He busted me a few times shoplifting years ago. So instead of arresting me he let me work it off in so many words," Shalonda confessed.

"Jeff" screamed Myshelle and Tiffany together.

"First he only let me perform oral sex on him in his police car. Then I got busted in Macy's for stealing a year back, the store wanted to press charges on me but he convinced the store manager that I was going to be put in a rehabilitative program for juvenile offenders. They didn't press charges and now I had graduated to having sex with him in his car. He never took me to a hotel, motel, nothing. Just some dark stank ass back alley."

"That dirty motherfucker," yelled Tiffany in horror.

"Wow is all I can say. You never really know what people have going on," lamented Myshelle.

"Oh my God, I can't even believe this...Jeff of all people."

"You think he has something to do with Prin being missing?"

"Maybe, maybe not. We're going to find out though."

CHAPTER IX:

JUSTICE...NOT MEANT TO BE NICE

Before Tiffany could immerse herself in her latest plan her cell phone was ringing. The number wasn't familiar but she answered it anyway, "Officer Saunders," she spoke. What Tiffany heard was almost as shocking and unsettling as finding the captured girls. Juice was dead. Tiffany sat in horror as she tried to process the latest turn of events.

"Damn," she muttered out loud.

"What's wrong?" asked Shalonda curiously from the kitchen.

"Juice is dead."

"What?" Shalonda screamed in horror.

"I just got the call. Apparently they found my number in his cell phone."

"How was he killed?"

"He was shot 3 times."

"Oh my God, you think this is because of ...?" asked Shalonda almost afraid of the impending response.

"Of course it is. The girls get freed, the Russians get locked up and now Juice is dead. Of course this is all connected. I've got to go check out the crime scene. Please stay here. Don't leave, don't answer the phone. Don't do anything but chill till either I get back or Myshelle gets back, okay?"

"Where am I supposed to go? And Juice dead. I don't want to get killed Tiffany."

"I'm going to protect you but I need you to stay here till I get back. I've got to see something," said Tiffany locking the door behind her as she left her house to head to the scene of the crime.

When Tiffany arrived on the scene at Juice's house according to the address on his driver's license police cruisers and officers were everywhere. He must have been on his way out when he was gunned down in his driveway next to his white BMW. A familiar face was walking the crime scene for clues. It was her ex-partner Jeff. How convenient thought Tiffany? She was definitely more suspicious because Jeff had no real reason to be on the scene. Tiffany was sure Jeff had some involvement with Juice's death and Princess disappearance. She just had no idea how to connect him to both crimes. Until she had proof she knew she had to play dumb and act as natural as possible.

She strolled behind Jeff as he examined the ground for shells, she tugged on the back of his shirt to get his attention. In an instant he spun around and enveloped Tiffany into tight embrace.

"Tiff what are you doing here?" Jeff asked curiously.

"I got a called because they found my number in his phone."

"How so?"

"I got a lead on Princess and I thought he had some information that could help me find her."

"Did he?"

"No, I think he was stringing me along because he was scared to death I was going to lock his ass up," she laughed.

"Damn."

"How do you know Juice?" she asked.

"Oh I busted him on some priors. Captain thought I might be able to provide some insight on what he was into before he was killed."

"You need help?"

"Not really. I thought you were supposed to be at home, not out here roaming the streets looking for clues. Let us do our job. You know we're the best at what we do, hell, you work with us."

"It's no way I can sit on my hands doing nothing. My baby is in danger and I know it."

"You don't know that. Have you eaten?"

"Nah, I don't have much of an appetite."

"Okay, I was going to take you to get something to eat. Get your mind off of all of this for a few," he smiled coyly.

"Thanks but I couldn't eat if I wanted to. I'm about to get out here and head back home. I've got to get some things straight with the Sargent and I'm out."

"Call me if you need anything," he offered.

"You know I will," she agreed.

Tiffany walked inside Juice's home looking for the Sargent on the scene. She found him talking to the Coroner and waited until he was finished before she took him to the side and explained why she had a dead man's number in his cell phone. The Sargent took her statement and sent her home. She had no place or purpose being at the crime scene and she wasn't certain there was any evidence that could help her. As she sat in her car pondering her next move she decided to try Princess telephone number again. Her heart lit up when it began ringing. Seconds later the phone was answered, "hello," said the female voice.

"This isn't Princess. Where's Princess?" asked Tiffany confused.

The phone hung up and rang busy when Tiffany tried to call it back. A light bulb must have gone off in her head because she remembered Princess' track my phone feature. She used the app on her phone to see if she could track the location of her daughter's phone. What she saw next was even more puzzling. Her daughter's phone tracked back to her precinct. Miffed Tiffany sped the whole way to her precinct ignoring traffic lights and pedestrians alike. She tracked the phone to a locked evidence room on the 2nd floor. She found Ellie, the officer in charge of processing the evidence in the break room down the hallway eating a sandwich.

"Ellie I need to talk to you, you have a minute," asked Tiffany out of breath.

"Sure, cop a squat," she said pulling out the chair next to her.

Tiffany sat down quickly with intent, "what is my daughter's phone doing in the evidence room?"

"Huh?" she asked dropping her sandwich on the plate.

"I called a few minutes ago and for the first time in days it rang, a woman answered and hung up. I tracked it while it was still on and it's showing that it's in the evidence room."

"Okay, sorry...I had no idea that was Princess phone. They haven't been processed yet. I just was charging up the phones to see if they work so they could be processed."

"How did it get here?"

"In a box of evidence that came from the Westham Parkway abduction cases. I'm so sorry I didn't correlate the names when you said Princess, plus I shouldn't have answered the phone but it caught me off guard. That's why I hung up so fast."

Tiffany was loss for words. Her heart was breaking more and more by the second.

"That is major. You need to tell the Captain. I'll corroborate the information," Ellie offered.

"I can't believe it. Those Russians must know where my daughter is. Are they still being held here?"

"I don't think so. I think they were transferred to Lockup."

"Shit, it's no way anyone is going to let me get in to talk to them."

"I'm sorry Tiffany. If there is something I can do, let me know."

"Yeah, this conversation never happened. We'll deal with this when it comes up. For now, just continue on with your processing and let me know if you find anything useful please?"

"Of course."

"Thanks Ellie," said Tiffany more determined to find out who was involved with her daughter's disappearance that would lead her to her daughter. Tiffany couldn't go down to the jail without it becoming questionable but she knew who would and could go down the jail to get some information. Tiffany called Myshelle's phone. She answered on the first ring, "what happened?"

"Princess phone was in the Russians house all along. It's now in the evidence room being processed. On that note I need you go to visit your brother."

"Jacky?"

"Yes, I need you to put Jacky onto these Russians for some information. If Princess phone was there, she was there. Can you do that for me?"

"Of course, I haven't seen Jack in months but I'll check him out first thing."

"Good. Are you back at my house yet?"

"Not yet I was just spending some time with Rod and the kids. I'm about to head back over."

"Just check on Shalonda for me. I don't want her to get any ideas and leave."

"Okay I'll text you an update in a minute. Where are you headed to now?"

"I don't know. I'm just tired. Scared. Pissed. Angry. All of the above."

I know but we're going to find her...alive."

"I hope so. I'll see you shortly though," said Tiffany trying to hold back the tears before hanging up. When Tiffany got back in her car she just sat there wanting to inflict all of her pain on someone or something but not having a clue who to hold responsible. Once she was able to drive she found herself at one of her daughter's favorite parks as a child, Abner Clay Park. She parked and just sat there staring at the playground being reminded of the days when her daughter was a young child engrossed in play. She longed for those days again.

Something compelled Tiffany to get out of her car and walk over to the swings that her daughter loved so much. She sat down in the swing and broke down in tears. Tiffany had no control over the river like flow of tears that ran down her face wetting her shirt. When she looked to the sky for answers an image of her daughter appeared.

"Where are you Princess?" sobbed Tiffany aloud as if she expected an answer.

She rocked back and forth slowly allowing her feet to drag in the gravel. Her head now hung low for fear of the worst. There had been no leads received from the Amber Alert. The police department that she worked and served didn't appear to be doing much about her daughter's disappearance and that hurt like a stab in the back. There was so much going on in Tiffany's heart. On one side there was the love of her daughter that kept her strong; on the other side it was her anger and rage that she wanted to inflict on whoever took her daughter away from her. Tiffany tried to fight what her mind was telling her...her daughter was dead. Why hadn't she turned up at the Russian's house? Maybe she fought back or tried to get away and was killed as a result.

Tiffany wailed like so many other brokenhearted mothers who were faced with the unimaginable task of burying their child. She tried to be strong but she felt weak and lifeless sitting on the swing seat. She sat there motionless for minutes that felt like hours. When she opened her eyes and looked back down at her feet, what appeared to be a ripped piece of a flyer was lying on the ground inches from her right foot, it read: Never give up. She took that as an intentional message to never stop looking for Princess, no matter what. The real question is what she would do with herself in the meantime.

Eventually Tiffany was able to pull herself away from the swings and the moment she was caught up in. Teary eyed but determined Tiffany headed home. Shalonda was certainly not her daughter but she was a young woman in need of help. There were many girls and women alike that probably needed her help too. Maybe she could help. Maybe there was something she could do. She retired for the evening to her house where Myshelle and Shalonda were sitting on the couch in the den watching television.

"You okay?" questioned Myshelle.

"Yeah just contemplating," Tiffany said falling into the cushions of the loveseat.

"Contemplating what?"

"Whether my daughter is dead or alive."

"We have to remain hopeful. Princess is alive and well."

"But if she isn't? What am I supposed to do?"

"Keep living."

"For what? Everything that I have ever done in my adult life has been for my daughter. To love her. To keep her safe. To give her opportunities. If I don't have my daughter I don't have any motivation or reason to do anything. I can't work like this. Maybe I'll end up a homeless wanderer," she lamented.

"Never that Tiff. Stay focused. We are going to find Princess and the people responsible for taking her."

"I guess I'm just trying to prepare myself for the worst."

"Tiffany I know you don't know me very well but I appreciate everything that you've been doing to help me. I know I can never replace Princess and would never try to but I don't have a mom. I'll be here for you," said Shalonda getting up to hug the worried mother.

"That's sweet. Thank you," Tiffany cried.

"You should get some rest. Your mind needs a break," ordered Myshelle.

"I would love to sleep right now but every time I close my eyes I see Princess."

"That shouldn't stop you from trying though."

"I guess. I'll try but I know it won't do any good," Tiffany surrendered. She left Myshelle and Shalonda to their television program and retired in her bedroom for the night. She took her clothes off and threw them on the floor before finding her comfy spot on the left side of her bed. Wrapped up in her covers she tried not to think about all the things she missed about her daughter other than her physical presence.

"God I know we don't talk enough. I know I don't even worship enough but even with my imperfections and flaws I know love because of you. You are love. You gave me love, my baby and I miss her so much right now. I'm praying she is safe and unharmed and if not I pray her soul is resting peacefully. Please help me find my daughter, your child, your precious gift to me. Help me to find her abductors and give me the strength to be merciful on them and their families. Give me the strength to forgive in the midst of my pain Lord. But most of all, give me my daughter back. Please Lord."

Tiffany sobbed herself asleep and woke up early before the sunrise. She opened her blinds and stared out at the sun as it rose above the horizon. She picked up her cell phone off the night stand and checked her voicemail and text messages. There were no new messages on either platform. She turned on her shower in her bathroom as her cell phone began ringing. She ran and answered it before it hung up, "Officer Saunders."

"Good Morning Beautiful," said Nigel.

"Morning Nigel."

"Still no Princess?" he asked.

"No, not at all and to top it off, the guy that was trying to help me was killed yesterday."

"What?"

"Yes, this has been one disaster after the next. And I still don't have a clue where my daughter is or who she is with."

"That's messed up."

"I'm so sorry Tiff."

"Thanks. I'm just trying to stay positive but every day that passes feels like a death sentence."

"I can't even begin to fathom what you're going through right now but I called because I miss you and I want to help. I've been trying to keep my distance to give you space to deal with this but I want to help. I can help."

"That's sweet but I don't even know where to begin."

"Lucky for me I have experience in this area. I reached out to my friends and family and explained to them what's going on with you. I have about 80 volunteers who will be ready in an hour for a search party around various areas."

"What?" she exclaimed in shock.

"Yes ma'am, I got your back and so do my people. Let us help you find your daughter."

Tears began to flow from Tiffany's eyes down her face and pajamas. She was speechless.

"I don't know what to say," she cried.

"Say you'll open the door and let me in. I'm outside."

Tiffany ran to her bedroom window and looked outside. Sure enough there was Nigel standing next to his car holding a dozen pink roses and a large bag from Panera. Tiffany waved at Nigel and then grabbed her robe from the back of her bedroom door and slid it on. She ran downstairs and opened the front door for him. He walked up and just hugged her for a minute. She pressed her face into his chest. His embrace made her feel secure and safe. Nigel was a good guy and she definitely wanted the opportunity to introduce him to the most important person in her life.

"Thank you," she whispered.

"You don't have to thank me. This is nothing. I wish there was more I can do."

"Come inside," she said pulling the sleeve of his shirt.

"Thank you. Would love to."

"What's in the bag?"

"Breakfast. Bagels, cream cheese, fruit and coffee."

"Hmm, I haven't had an appetite in days but I love those bagels," she said leading him through the den into the kitchen. Myshelle and Shalonda were fast asleep on the floor.

"That's your friend from the bar," he asked confused.

"Yeah. We're good now."

"Good to hear."

Tiffany retrieved two plates and two coffee mugs from the kitchen cabinets. She rinsed them off and dried them with paper towels as he took the food out of the bag.

"You have a vase?" he asked.

"Over there in that cabinet," she pointed.

"Okay," he said opening the cabinet and finding a pretty vase to put the flowers in. He found the cutting shears on the counter and began cutting each rose on a slant and placing it in the vase with the flower food.

Tiffany watched with delight as Nigel made himself comfortable in her home. He even looked good at it and like be belonged there. In her fantasy world the only thing that was missing was Princess. She would like Nigel, more importantly she would like the fact that Nigel liked Tiffany.

"So you've had your hands busy organizing this search party huh?" she asked.

"Not really. That was easy."

"Okay, excuse me," she joked.

"What's going to be hard is planning that next date," he flirted.

"Why?"

"Because I want to make sure you have the time of your life."

"That sounds good but I can't even think about a real date right now. Of course I want to see you but I can't go anywhere for leisure right now and enjoy it."

"I know. That's why I'm saving our next date for after Princess is back."

"You're hopeful huh?"

"Of course."

Tiffany just stared at him amazed at his thoughtfulness.

"You feel too good to be true."

Nigel pinched her.

"Ouch," she whined.

"At least you're not dreaming."

"Funny, ha ha," she said pinching his butt playfully.

"Ooh la la," he laughed.

When Tiffany turned her back to pick up the prepared plates he started tickling her on her sides till she almost dropped the plates. Quickly he grabbed the plates and set them down on the dining room table and then grabbed Tiffany's elbow to pull her in for a kiss. She retreated and melted in his arms kissing him back. When they pulled away from their embrace Myshelle was standing there watching them like a lovesick puppy.

"Ah, that is so cute," Myshelle commented.

"Good Morning," beamed Tiffany smiling like a love struck teen caught by their parent.

"Morning," piped Nigel.

"Well well well, what did I miss while I was asleep?" Myshelle teased.

"Nothing and everything. I got a little bit of rest though it doesn't feel like it and Nigel surprised me with breakfast and flowers this morning...and he organized a search party for Princess today."

"I did miss a lot. That is awesome. Thanks Nigel," said Myshelle helping herself to one of the bagels.

"You're welcome. You want some coffee?" he asked.

"Certainly," Myshelle said taking a seat at the kitchen island.

"Here you go," he said pouring the coffee into one of the mugs before getting another one out of the cabinet.

"Such a gentleman. He's a keeper Tiff."

"That's what I'm talking about," shouted Nigel.

"Ssshh, Shalonda is still asleep," laughed Tiffany.

"Oh that's right, I'm sorry. I forgot there was someone else here. By the way who is she?"

"Well the short of it is that Shalonda was one of the last people with Princess before she disappeared."

"Okay so is she here voluntarily or ...?"

"It's voluntarily now," Tiffany said matter of factly.

"I see. You gotta do what you gotta do," Nigel remarked.

"Amen to that," chimed Myshelle delightfully while eating her bagel.

"I know this is all last minute for you but the volunteers should be meeting me at the site in an hour and a half."

"I'm going to run home and shower. I'll be back in an hour," said Myshelle leaving with her plate and mug in hand.

"She just took the plate and cup huh?" he laughed.

"Yep but at least I don't have to go far to get it."

"True."

"Well I have to go upstairs and shower. You can join me upstairs and watch some tv in my room while I get ready?"

"Hell yes," he said grabbing Tiffany by the arm pretending to drag her upstairs.

"Boy you are too much," she laughed playfully as she allowed herself to be led upstairs to her room.

"Which room is yours?"

"That one," she pointed.

"Nice," he said as he walked into her bedroom.

"Is it everything you thought it would be?" she asked coyly.

"You or the room?"

"Me first, then the room."

"You are the bomb.com which would be more than I ever could expected or feel I'm worthy of. The room is nice too though."

"When this is all over I want you to have dinner with us, so you can officially meet Princess."

"Looking forward to it, now get your butt into high gear so we can go find her and have dinner tonight."

"I like how you think," she blushed.

For the first time in days Tiffany felt hopeful that all would be good again soon and just maybe there was hope for her blossoming little family.

CHAPTER X:

THE SEARCH IS ON

Tiffany got dressed as fast as she could with Nigel distracting her. They had a really good chemistry and vibe that Tiffany hadn't felt with anyone in years. She truly enjoyed his company even under the current circumstances she found herself in. He was a refreshing change of pace that kept her distracted enough from killing herself with stress. Tiffany didn't have the time or patience to put a lot of thought into second guessing herself and her judgment of people including Nigel. She tried not to blame herself for her daughter's disappearance. Never in a million years did Tiffany ever consider that something like this could happen to her daughter. Working in law enforcement didn't even prepare her for this. Yet she knew the why didn't really matter; it just mattered that she got her daughter back...at any costs. Right about now she had wished there was a ransom or opportunity to reason or satisfy any requirement that assured her daughter's safe return. That would be easy. Being completely in the dark and oblivious to your child's vanishing was the worst heart wrenching soul killing feeling she had ever experienced. This she wished on no one, not even her worst enemy.

Tiffany dressed comfortably in her favorite old jeans and sneakers. She found a comfortable white sweater in the back of her closet and put it on over her jeans. It was definitely a ponytail day. She tried to use what energy and strength she had on necessary tasks not trivial things like styling her hair or wearing makeup. As much as she wanted to try to be cute for Nigel that was not even on her radar and she truly felt like with him it didn't matter. Tiffany was ready in great time, with time to spear en route to the meeting site. She called Will and Cindy to let them know about the search efforts that was organized for Princess. They agreed to meet them at the site within the hour to participate.

When Tiffany and Nigel returned to the first floor Shalonda was now wide awake while and Myshelle was dressed and ready to go. "Good Morning," Shalonda said extending her arms to give Tiffany a hug.

"Morning Shalonda. This is my friend Nigel. Nigel this is Shalonda, this is one of Princess' friends that has been helping me look for her," Tiffany explained.

"Nice to meet you," said Nigel shaking the young woman's hand.

"Thanks," Shalonda said confused about what to say.

"We're getting ready to leave. Nigel is a fellow officer who went out of his way to organize a search party for Prin that starts shortly," Tiffany further explained.

"That's good. Okay, do I have enough time to get ready really quick?" Shalonda asked.

"Truthfully I didn't think it was a good idea for you to go. You never know who might see you with us, I don't want to compromise all the work we've put in lately."

"What? I've got to stay here...alone?"

"Yes but I can have Myshelle's daughter Tyshelle come over to keep you company."

"That's nice but I really want to help with the search. What if I wear a disguise?"

"A disguise. What kind of disguise?"

"I don't know. Just give me a hat with a brim and some dark sunglasses. Nobody will recognize me. I promise. I will keep my head down and stay out the way. Please just don't leave me here," Shalonda begged.

"I don't know," contemplated Tiffany.

"Me and Tyshelle will keep our eye on her at the search," offered Myshelle.

"See, she will look out for me. I'll stay with her and everything will be alright."

"Girl I hope so. You gotta hurry up and get ready though. We were just about to leave," Tiffany said.

"Yes ma'am, all I need is 5 minutes. I'll be right back," she said trampling upstairs to the bathroom.

"How about we finish our coffee while we wait," suggested Nigel.

"Sounds good," replied Tiffany.

Myshelle handed Nigel and Tiffany their coffee mugs and continued blushing at the potential couple.

"Why are you looking so goofy?" Tiffany asked Myshelle.

"Just admiring you two. Y'all make a cute couple," Myshelle stated.

"I shouldn't have asked," said Tiffany directing her attention to Nigel, "I'm sorry about my friend."

"For what? I think she was dead on accurate. We do make a cute couple," he said shooting Myshelle a high five.

"Oh I see what's happening here," Tiffany smiled to herself.

The antics of Nigel and Myshelle were interrupted by Shalonda's speedy return downstairs. She was fully dressed modestly, hair pulled back into a bun and looking like her actual age. For a second she almost looked like Princess. Maybe it was because she was wearing Princess' clothes thought Tiffany. A closer look revealed similar physical body and facial characteristics between the two girls. Maybe she was hallucinating and just wanting to see her daughter in Shalonda. Tiffany put the thought in the back of her head and assumed she was reaching.

"You look cute," complimented Tiffany.

"Thanks, I figured it was okay since I don't have a change of clothes here," Shalonda explained.

"Of course it's fine. Help yourself to whatever is in her closet, I know she wouldn't mind at all...okay she would at first but then not really."

"It looks like we're all ready to go," Nigel jumped up clapping his hands together.

"Awesome, let's go," said Tiffany.

The group headed to the door behind Tiffany. She locked up her house and they were on their way. They were three cars deep leaving the neighborhood. Nigel lead the group out, as Myshelle followed him and TyRod followed his wife.

The command center of the search party wasn't far from Will's house. A friend of Nigel's was able to secure them use of a mason's lodge in the area. Traffic spilled out onto the main road from the lodge. So many people had turned out in short notice to help search for Princess. Tiffany was moved to tears at the sight of so many people there to help. Myshelle rubbed Tiffany's back to console her.

"This is amazing," remarked Shalonda cloaked in discreet dark large frame sunglasses.

"Yes it is," agreed Myshelle navigating through the hoard of people. She continued to follow Nigel to reserved parking that had been roped off near the lodge.

"You think he knows all these people?" Shalonda asked.

"Nine times out of ten, yes," said Tiffany.

Nigel was parked and out of his car quickly. He popped his trunk open and started pulling boxes out and setting them on the ground next to his parked car. Myshelle parked closely next to him to allow space for TyRod's big truck and another car if necessary.

"What's in the boxes?" asked Tiffany.

"T-shirts and flyers."

"What?" she asked stunned.

"I had some flyers and t-shirts made," Nigel stated.

"I cannot believe you. How did you even do all of this? Why would you do all of this?"

"Why wouldn't I do this? Anybody would have done the same thing. Lucky for me I'm in law enforcement and have way more experience with this than I care to...but I thank God I have this training, knowledge in experience because now I can use it to help someone that I really care about."

"You continue to amaze me."

"That's a compliment. Thank you. Now if you really want to thank me, grab a box so we can get this search party started."

"Let's," she said grabbing the box off the top and following Nigel to two long tables flanked by fold up chairs. At the table all the introductions and pleasantries were exchanged amongst the group as Will arrived. He must have brought the whole crew because he was driving his Benz Sprinter van.

Tiffany sprinted over to the van to show him where he could park. Will and his crew of 11 piled out of the van looking like a basketball team. He had brought the whole family. Will and Tiffany hugged, and then she hugged Cindy and all the kids. She offered to introduce him to her friend that organized the search party. More greetings and hugs were exchanged before the search party officially got underway.

Nigel was organized and efficient in passing out assignments to the crew organized to run the command center. The volunteers had formed lines to receive supplies at one table. Supplies on the first table included fliers, t-shirts, flash lights, walkie talkies, name tags, markers, and a bull horn. The second table had been set up buffet style with refreshments, beverages, condiments and plates, cups and cutlery. On that table were trays of bagels and different flavor cream cheeses, muffins and Danish pastries, fruit trays with fruit dip, juices, milks and coffee.

Tiffany was in utter disbelief. Everything was so well organized and generous. Nigel had paid for all of the food and supplies out of his own money. The fliers and t-shirts were donated by friends of his. There was just so much thought and preparation put into the whole effort and Tiffany was blown away that Nigel would do something of this magnitude for her and Princess. She had a good feeling about the search and was feeling positive about what lay ahead of them. She jumped right into things helping out wherever she could, Nigel hadn't given her any assignment because he wanted her to be at the command center on standby if necessary. Before she knew it she was passing out drinks, making sure people had napkins, more coffee, fliers. She answered questions about her daughter's like's, friends and lifestyle.

Nigel had already determined six areas all over the city that would send volunteers off in individual groups to scour the area while passing out flier's door to door. The fliers had a direct hot line to Nigel's cell phone for tips or information. Before dismissing the volunteers to their assignments Nigel asked them all to gather for a prayer. He asked Will to give them a word before they departed. Will smiled and happily obliged.

"Let us bow our heads in prayer please people. Father God thank you for assembling us all here today on behalf of my daughter Princess. We thank you for Nigel and his friends who put aside their personal lives and dealings to help us recover what was taken from us. We ask that you guide each of our volunteers today, guide their hearts, minds and souls. Protect us and reveal to us anything that could bring us closer to finding Princess. In Jesus Name we pray, Amen."

"Amen," they all said in unison.

Nigel then directed the group leaders to disperse the groups and advised them of the check in and lunch in four hours. Tiffany was now at the table writing out name tags for people, shaking hands and greeting people. She thanked everyone for their time and support and wished them a safe search. The search was well underway as the volunteers piled in cars together to complete their search assignment. Tiffany, Myshelle, Shalonda and the rest of the group manned the tables. There were even news reporters with their cameramen and crews on the scene of the search party. Nigel had truly outdone himself. This had to lead to some good solid leads that could help them find Princess.

As time flew by Nigel's phone rang every few minutes with bits and pieces of information. There was a group that canvassed the motel Princess was last seen at with Juice. One of the occupants of the motel alleged that they saw Princess walk to the bus stop and get on a GRTC bus. All the information received via the hotline was logged in a notebook with contact information for the witness with the details of the sighting. Tiffany was pleased at the information that was coming in. Only time would tell how credible it would actually be.

As the time wound down and it got closer to check in time, Tiffany found herself being interviewed by the reporters for various news outlets. She gave a description and the telephone number to the hotline for any tips or information that would aid them in finding her daughter. The taped segments were going to be aired on the six o' clock news. Feeling a little flushed after speaking with so many people in a short time Tiffany decided to go inside of the lodge to get away from some of the crowd. It had almost gotten a little overwhelming. She could feel the overflow of emotion like a tidal wave and was doing all she could to control it and be as pleasant and helpful as possible. She definitely didn't want to seem ungrateful.

Tiffany decided to excuse herself to the restroom to throw some cold water on her face. Surely that would help her get the wind back beneath her sails. She found solace leaning all her weight on the inside of a bathroom stall as she steadied herself. There was a nauseating feeling that hit her unexpectedly causing her to try to keep her balance. She didn't want to pass out and hit the floor. That would only make the day more dramatic. She wanted to remain in control as much as possible. She wanted to feel strong. The minute she started to cave in mentally to her inner feelings it would be a losing battle from that point.

Stuff like this didn't happen to people like her. Tiffany had done everything as right as possible with Princess. Always trying to give her the things

233

she needed, wanted and then some. Setting her up for a bright future is what Tiffany believed she was doing as a single mother. She began to question whether she had put her career before her daughter and now it had cost her. Maybe it was her fault that Princess was gone. Tiffany had put such emphasis on ensuring that the bills were paid that she had taken on more overtime trying to make as much money as possible. There were many evenings where Princess was alone. Tiffany didn't want to blame herself but everything pointed to her. She certainly couldn't help but feel that way.

She had to shake the defeatist depressing thoughts that were running through her head. She tried to think of images of strength for motivation and she ran blank. Her tank was empty. She was long ago making it by on fumes. Now she was just totally out and she couldn't make herself move. Tiffany started to weep as she tried to regain control of her body and mind. She was falling apart mentally and physically. What was it going to take to get her out of the bathroom stall and not stretched out on the floor? As she closed her eyes to pray the bathroom door swung open and someone walked in. Thank God thought Tiffany.

"Excuse me, I need some help. This search party is for my daughter and I'm not feeling well and can't move, can you please help me?" she cried.

"Oh yes yes, yes ma'am," said a woman from the other side of the bathroom stall. She tried to push on the door but it was locked. Thinking quickly, she got on the floor and crawled underneath the door. She saw Tiffany leaning headfirst into the wall in agony. The lady unlocked the stall door and leaned Tiffany against her body as she maneuvered her out of the bathroom slowly. As she was struggling to get her to the door another woman walked in and immediately helped the woman with Tiffany. They carried her out to a chair in the main hall and propped her feet up in another chair.

The first lady ran to get Nigel to call for emergency response. Nigel dashed in like a true hero ready to save the day. He took Tiffany's pulse and pulled the walkie talkie off his waistband and radioed for an ambulance. The paramedics arrived promptly and had Tiffany on the stretcher and on her way to the hospital in no time. Myshelle rode in the ambulance with her so that Nigel could stay and continue to manage the search party. Myshelle prayed frantically as she watched the EMS team check her best friend's blood pressure and heart rate.

At the hospital Tiffany was admitted for severe dehydration, anxiety and depression. She was given certain drugs to stabilize her mental state and an IV to replenish her fluids. Hours after the search ended Tiffany woke up in a cloud like fog. Everything looked hazy and muddled. Truth was she had been in such a depressed and downtrodden state of mind she couldn't tell if her present condition was natural or onset because of the medicine the doctors had given her. She wasn't too high to forget about Princess search party and the results it yielded. Hard pressed to know what happened Tiffany tried to get off the hospital bed but was stopped by the many wires and machines she was hooked up too. As she tried to disconnect the wires an alarm was set off in her room causing the nurses to flood her room to check her status.

"Ma'am, please stay in your bed," the older black nurse requested.

"I've got to get out of here. I need to find out what happened to my daughter's search party. She's been missing for a week now. Please help me," cried Tiffany as she grabbed the woman's hands in mercy.

"You're the officer whose daughter has been missing?"

"Yes ma'am, I was at the search party and I must have passed out or something. I just need to know what happened."

"Okay, do me a favor and sit back in the bed. I'll go to the nurses' station and see what I can find out. You had some folks hanging around while you slept. They may still be in the building."

"Do you know who it was?"

"I didn't get a name, it was a woman and two men."

"Okay, thank you ma'am."

"No problem, just let us take care of you so you can get out here and go get your baby back."

"That's exactly what I want to do."

"No problem, I'll be right back," the nurse said leaving the room and closing the door behind her.

Tiffany fidgeted in her bed as she waited for the nurse to return, when her patience began to run dry she began looking for the phone that was customary in most hospital rooms. With no phone Tiffany had to calm her nerves as best she could and wait. Lord knows she didn't want to end up committed in the psych ward with no ability to help her daughter.

The door to her room swung open and in walked Myshelle, TyRod and Will.

"You're awake Sunshine," said Myshelle going to her best friend's side to hug her.

"Yes but what happened? Tell me we got some good leads. Where's Nigel?"

"Whoa, slow down," suggested Myshelle.

"How long have I been in here?"

"First things first. Nigel is at the precinct passing on the leads we received off the hotline today. I can't say how credible the information was but it's all being checked into right now," Myshelle updated.

"Who did he pass the information on to?"

"Jeff."

"No! No! Oh God he shouldn't have done that!"

"Why not?" asked Will concerned.

"Something is up with him. I believe he had something to do with it, and if he didn't...he's involved somehow. I was going to share my concerns with Nigel today but of course I never got the chance."

"You don't really think he had something to do with Princess disappearance?" TyRod inquired.

"I can't say for sure but I just have this feeling. Something isn't right about him."

"What do you need us to do?" asked Myshelle.

"Get me out of here."

"I'll go talk to the doctors," Will offered and left the room.

"Where's Shalonda?"

"She's at my house with the kids."

"Good. I'm so hungry right now. My head is banging. Lord I need a miracle."

"Well my name ain't Miracle but I got your back," said Myshelle reaching into her large bright red hand bag. She pulled out a sandwich, chips, a Snapple, the corded phone that was missing from her room, her cell phone, a pair of pajamas and bedroom slippers. Tiffany smiled.

"You're the best."

"I know, that's why I'm your bestie!"

Myshelle plugged the phone back into the wall and pulled the bed tray over and opened up the food for Tiffany to eat.

"It smells good. I just don't know if I can eat it."

"Just try. If you don't finish it Rod will."

"I sure will," he agreed leaned against the wall.

Tiffany said a silent prayer before picking up the sandwich to take a bite. She washed it down with the Snapple and nibbled a bit more before wrapping it back up in the foil. She wiped her hands on a napkin and began checking her phone for messages and emails as Will walked back in the room followed by a team of doctors.

"Officer Saunders good to see you awake, and it looks like you're coming around nicely. Is that my lunch?" the young looking black male doctor asked jokingly.

"It can be if you can release me."

"Hand that sandwich over then, you're getting out of here soon."

"Thank you so much," she said handing him the half eaten sandwich.

"I was kidding. Enjoy your food. Nice gesture of you though but really your vital signs are stable. I'm Doctor Shahid, I've been monitoring you since you were admitted. You got plenty of fluids while you rested. There's no reason medically to keep you. Now I will say that I heard about what's going on with your daughter. I'm sorry to hear that and I pray you find her soon. In the meantime, your stress levels are considerably high and I need you to take it easy as much as possible over the next few days while you bounce back from this episode. I'm prescribing you Xanax. You need help managing the anxiety and stress right now. Do I think you need to take this long term? No. I want you to follow up with your primary in a week and discontinue the Xanax when your stress levels have returned to a somewhat normal level."

"Yes sir. Thank you. I appreciate it."

"Also, I was hoping it was okay if I could just pray with you for your daughter?" he asked.

Tiffany's eyes lit up in surprise, "Certainly".

The doctor set his clipboard down on the bed and walked over to the bed where he took Tiffany's hands inside his. He closed his eyes and began to speak rivers of living water over Tiffany and her daughter. He prayed for her safe return to her family and for justice to be done. When he was done they all agreed with, "Amen".

"Thanks doctor."

"You're very welcome. I wish you the best. Nice meeting you folks again. If I can be of assistance, please let me know. I'll send the nurse in with the discharge papers," he said before leaving.

"Thank you," said Myshelle as she packed the pajamas and slippers back into her bag since Tiffany wouldn't be staying long enough to need them.

The nurse interrupted them and began explaining the discharge instructions and medication she was being prescribed. Tiffany tried to listen but her mind was elsewhere. She just nodded in agreement and thanked the woman for her help. Once she had been unhooked from the machines Will helped Tiffany out of the bed and then gave her a hug. He was already worried about Princess, now he wasn't sure how Tiffany would hold up under the current circumstances.

"I'm so sorry Tiffany," Will broke down crying.

"For what?"

"All of this happened on my watch. The minute I was supposed to be building a relationship with our daughter this happens and I can't help but feel like this is my fault. I never meant to let anything happen to her," he sobbed.

"Will this isn't your fault. Is that what you think? That I blame you for this," she asked.

"I would. I do."

"This is nobody's fault. Not even Princess fault. I have no idea what she was doing that caused this to happen but even she couldn't have seen this coming."

"I'm so scared Tiffany," he confessed.

"I am too," she confirmed.

CHAPTER XI:

LOVE, A LEAD & HEARTBREAK

Back in the comforts of her home Tiffany was anything but comfortable. She waited patiently for Nigel to call her back with some kind of update. Shalonda was still at Myshelle's house getting some much needed time with peers her own age. She had actually been enjoying herself and for the first time in years she felt like a true teenager. She didn't have to worry about where she was going to sleep or what she was going to eat. She didn't even have to worry about what illicit acts she would have to perform to eat or sleep safely. Patience was never one of Tiffany's true virtues it was something she had learned to harness when needed over the years. After her fourth call to Nigel with no return call Tiffany decided to just relax as best she could. Even if she wanted to get out and search Myshelle would have stopped her and she wouldn't have had a clue where to start. Juice was dead. She had no leads. She felt like she was stuck on a dead end.

As she treaded back and forth across the carpet in her den Nigel's car pulled up out front of her house. She beat him to the door and walked right into his arms. He kissed her on her forehead before walking arm in arm inside with her.

"So Joe what do you know?" she joked.

"You should sit down," he said somberly.

"Why?" she panicked.

"There may have been a sighting. Someone reported that they saw a girl that matched Princess description in the passenger side of a white Ford Taurus heading north on 95. The tipster said that it didn't appear that she girl looked distressed or like she was being held against her will. There was a partial plate number provided but no description of the driver. We've been checking DMV for cars that may match the description and partial plate. In the interim I got with your Captain to find out what they recovered from her phone. Apparently Princess was corresponding with someone she thought was her age. This guy reached out to her via her Facebook profile and they had been Snapchatting up until two days before she disappeared. So we are trying to nail down who this person is but it's a blind profile. No information, no profile. No posts just private messages to Princess," he revealed.

"Oh my God, I had no idea. How could this have happened? I check her phone constantly. I've never seen any snapchat app's or anything out of the ordinary on her phone."

"Some apps delete the history or she may have been removing the app prior to your checks so you wouldn't find it," Nigel informed them.

"I can't believe this. Why would she do that?" questioned Tiffany.

"Tiffany you and I both know you don't need a reason to do something stupid, you just do. We were that age once. Do you remember the things we did without our parent's knowledge?" Myshelle reminded Tiffany.

"Yeah but things were drastically different then."

"That's true."

"As soon as we get a match on the plate me and a couple of my partners are going to follow up on it."

"Did you talk to Jeff?"

"Yes...not that it matters but did you ever had a relationship or something with that dude?"

"Not a relationship. It was more of a fling of sorts. It was a long long time ago. He was my partner when I joined the police department. Why?"

"I just got a weird vibe from him at the search party. He seemed very on edge. He seemed like he was trying to help but then I got the feeling he was fishing for something. So I'm having somebody I know tail him for a couple of days."

"Whew, thank God. I was hoping it wasn't just me. That's all I was worried about in the hospital."

"My mama ain't raise no fool, that's for sure. But I feel good that we're going to find her. Soon."

"I hope so. Everyday she's gone a piece of me feels like it dies."

"I can't even imagine but I'm here. I'm not going anywhere."

"That makes me feel a little better."

"Have you eaten since you been back?" he asked concerned.

"I had a piece of a sandwich at the hospital but you know my appetite is nowhere right now."

"I was going to pick up some food, you want to ride with me. Get some fresh air?" he offered.

"Sure."

Tiffany took Nigel up on his offer to ride to get food. She needed a mental break from it all and she felt a lot better knowing that Nigel had too picked up on her own suspicions of Jeff. She trusted that even if her department and Jeff weren't making any strides in finding Princess she took comfort knowing that Nigel was on her side. Clearly he was using any resources available to him to help her. The ride was quiet. She didn't have a lot to say. She just needed to be in his presence. Tiffany thought about what her life looked like without her daughter. As much as she wanted to be hopeful for a good outcome she already felt like she had been given a death sentence. What if she had to face the fact that she may never see her daughter alive again? That was an unfortunate truth for many people with loved ones missing or presumed dead.

When Nigel saw Tiffany locked in a gaze as he drove, he grabbed her hand and squeezed it tight. She looked over at him and smiled. She thought about what type of relationship she could even have with Nigel under the circumstances? Would he still want to be with her after everything she had been through? Could she even love again? Thinking about all of it made her incredibly sad. She'd do anything to get her daughter back and move forward in her life. For now, she was stuck. She tried to put her faith in God as Will had advised her repeatedly but her faith was crumbling more daily. Still they retrieved the Chinese food and headed back to Tiffany house where Nigel ate and watched Tiffany fall asleep on the couch.

When Tiffany woke she was covered with a blanket as Nigel slept on the loveseat across from her. It was nice waking up to a man in her house but it would have been nicer if Princess were back home. Tiffany stretched her long legs out in front of her and proceeded to get up to put on a pot of coffee. Days like this she definitely needed coffee. Just as she crossed the threshold into the kitchen there was a quiet knock at her backdoor. Thinking it was Princess she ran to the door and flung it open. It was Shalonda.

"Hey girl. I thought you were Princess for a second," said Tiffany letting her in.

"I'm sorry. I just wanted to come check on you. I was having such a good time with Tyshelle and those crazy brothers of hers that I lost track of time and the reason I'm here."

"Shalonda you were doing exactly what a young girl your age should be doing. There's not a whole lot we can do with the information we have. Truly it's a waiting game at this point."

"Well is there something I can do. I did a load of towels yesterday and folded them up. I took the trash out and cleaned the downstairs bathroom. I know you don't have no time for that right now and I wanted to show you that I appreciate what you're doing for me, all while you're going through this with your daughter."

"Aww thanks sweetie. You didn't have to clean. I would have gotten to it...eventually."

"I know but I didn't mind."

"Thank you," she said opening her arms to hug Shalonda.

For a moment she hugged Shalonda like she was Princess. Oh how she missed her daughter terribly. Was Shalonda supposed to be a replacement?

"Myshelle fixed breakfast this morning. She's bringing you a plate over in a few."

"And to think I was going to fix you breakfast this morning. I miss fixing Princess her breakfast in the morning before school."

"You're a good mom Tiffany. I know she misses you too. I miss her myself. I'm just sorry she got caught up in some bull," Shalonda said.

"By the way did you know who Princess was snapchatting with? They found some deleted apps and conversations that showed Princess had been talking to a guy online before she disappeared."

"She had mentioned some guy from her class that she liked but that's about it."

"Figures, it appears that my child was harboring some secrets."

"We all do though."

"That is true. I haven't had a lot of time to talk to you the last couple of days but I really appreciate everything you've done to help me. I mean 110% that you can stay as long as you need to. I'm not trying to replace Princess with you but I can't send you back into the world you've been in. If you're going to be staying here I need to get you back in school. I want you to start thinking about your future and when you're ready I want you to mentor other young girls. Does that sound like something you can do?"

"Of course, that's easy. I mean, I miss school kind of anyways. It's just hard trying to keep up with grades and papers and stuff while you trying to work in the clubs."

"I know but I want this change to be a fresh start for you. You don't ever have to go back to your grandfather...ever. He shouldn't be allowed to hurt you or use you anymore. Okay."

"Yes ma'am," she nodded in agreement.

"Good well later today I want to get you settled in my guest room. That's your room from here on out. Decorate it how you please, all I ask is that you keep it clean and keep food from upstairs."

"I can do that."

"I knew you could. I'm not going to even lie; my shower is calling me. If Nigel wakes up let him know I'm in my room okay?"

"Yes ma'am...thank you again Tiffany."

"Your welcome sweetie. I'll be back down in a few," she said climbing the stairs to the second floor slowly.

Inside the safe confines of her bathroom Tiffany ran the hottest shower she could tolerate. The steam filled up the room and fogged up the mirrors. For a while she just stood in the vapors breathing it in and out. It was going to be hard living without Princess but something told Tiffany that she might as well get used to life as it was. A few minutes into her shower the door opened and Nigel let himself in.

"Can I come in?" he asked as he closed the door behind him.

"Sure, I could use some company. If it's not too hot for you come on in," she offered.

"I don't even know how to take that. It ain't never too hot for me," he joked stripping down to his birthday suit.

"You silly, you know what I meant."

"Got damn this water hot," he screeched as he joined her in the shower.

"Aww, I'm sorry," Tiffany laughed as she adjusted the water temperature.

"That's much better," he said relaxing his flinched muscles to allow the water to run down his body.

"Can you wash my back?"

"Hell yeah I can," he confirmed eagerly.

Tiffany handed him her soaped up wash cloth. Nigel washed her back sensually. He painted a soapy masterpiece on her back before letting the rag slide across her buttocks and down her legs. He turned Tiffany around to face him and began to wash her chest, then breasts and stomach. When the rag reached her navel he dropped the rag on the floor of the shower stall. He kneeled down in front of Tiffany and put her left leg over his shoulder. He locked eyes with her before she closed her eyes and leaned back onto the stall. He buried his face between her legs as the water ran down his back. Nigel drew soft circles with his tongue causing Tiffany to moan softly. Instantly she felt more relaxed than she could remember feeling in weeks. Nigel's oral exploration was tender and loving. He was a gentle and generous lover taking his time arousing Tiffany more and more with each kiss. She held on to the back of his head as the waves of orgasm crashed over her and completely overtook her. Satisfied with his performance Tiffany took her leg down from his shoulder and pulled him up to kiss her. There was so much unbridled passion and lust amongst them. Nigel's hands explored the rest of Tiffany's body while they kissed passionately in the shower. "I want you so bad," he moaned into her ear.

"I want you too."

"I have a condom in my wallet?"

"Get it."

Nigel opened the shower door and picked up his pants off the floor. He pulled his wallet out of his back pocket and retrieved the Magnum wrapper from inside. He tore into the packaging before sliding it on. When he turned around to go back in the shower stall Tiffany was standing behind him. She sat on top of her vanity and sink and gestured for Nigel to come closer. She pulled him into her and they became one. Nigel made love to Tiffany on her sink counter and it was everything and more that they both had hoped that it would be.

"So does this mean I'm your boyfriend?" Nigel asked playfully.

"Do you want to be my boyfriend?"

"I want to be your friend, lover, boyfriend, future baby daddy, husband..."

"So I guess that means its official."

"Well well well, it's been a long time since I had a girlfriend. You sure this is not too much in the midst of all this?"

"No, I need you Nigel...not for the sex, although that was amazing. I just need your companionship and support, and some love."

"I've got all that and more for you."

"I know you do, that's why I don't want to let you go. Everything about us feels right, even now amongst this storm that I'm in."

"I just want to be here for you. You shouldn't have to go through this alone. I'll always be here for you and Princess and I know that soon we are all going to be one big happy family."

"That would be nice."

Tiffany didn't know if she had jumped the gun by getting into a relationship with Nigel but she had to trust her gut. Everybody around Tiffany had somebody they could lean on during difficult situations. Myshelle had her husband. Will had his wife. Tiffany had nobody up until now. Of course she wasn't going to blab about her relationship to the world but she did take comfort in knowing that she wasn't alone anymore. The new couple finished their shower together and got dressed to start their day.

When they got back downstairs Tiffany wanted to turn the television for a distraction but she opted against it. Every time she watched television there was a new report of a missing child, murder investigation or a new instance of police brutality. It all proved to be a bit much for Tiffany who was eventually put on medical leave.

The hours turned into days, the days turned into weeks and those turned into months with no signs or contact from Princess. The leads in her case went cold. There were no answers for Tiffany who had grown more withdrawn and depressed daily. It was an awful existence to live in, a sort of paranormal universe. Tiffany had become a recluse only going outside when she needed to. Essentially she was hiding from the world, hiding from her deepest fear. Her relationship with Nigel dissolved during the months that followed. Her emotions had become unstable at best and even though Nigel did his best to comfort

Tiffany ultimately she pushed him away. The more she concluded that Princess was dead, the more she wanted to withdraw from the world. Initially she thought that she could muster the strength to love Nigel in spite of her loss but that proved to be too difficult for her.

Her days now consisted of searching online classifieds and profiles for possible leads to her daughter's whereabouts. Tiffany had seen so many children and young women caught up in underground sex trafficking rings for years, some for the rest of their lives. It broke Tiffany's heart to even consider that her daughter had gotten mixed up into something so horrible but it was a possibility. She had to consider all the possibilities at this point. It didn't matter what she thought actually happened to Princess, it all felt the same, incredibly painful, scary, soul wrenching and hurtful. It had been months since her daughter went missing. She tried to cling to hope and remain faithful that she would see her daughter again. Everything proved to be hard these days, even the simple things like having faith.

Tiffany sat at her kitchen counter fully immersed in her daily investigative work towards her daughter's case. With so much free time on her hands Tiffany made the most of it by trying to search online for evidence her daughter may be alive. Being out on medical leave made it difficult to truly monitor what was happening with her daughter's case. Jeff checked in with her from time to time saying nothing more than he "was still working on it". Tiffany knew there was something shady going on she just had no idea how to prove it.

The timer on the kitchen oven beeped snapping Tiffany out of her zone. She jumped up to turn the timer off and the oven. Tiffany grabbed her oven mitts and removed the hot cookie tray from the oven. She sat it down on the counter on top of a folded dish towel. Her chocolate chip cookies looked delicious. All that time around the house also became the driving force behind Tiffany's newfound love of baking. Make no mistakes Tiffany still didn't like to cook but she had fallen in love with baking. It had become very soothing and relaxing for her. Plus, she had a sweet tooth that was out of this world. It seemed to amplify when Princess disappeared. Baking and working out vigorously to keep all the sugar she consumed off was also a part of Tiffany's new life.

She knew this so called calm she perpetrated was a façade that was going to come tumbling down eventually. So she did the best she could to immerse herself in things that kept her mind occupied and doing something constructive. It didn't hurt that everybody benefited from her new hobby. There were always treats laying around and given away by Tiffany. She usually baked a lot more than she could actually eat or wanted to eat. She had even begun taking cakes and pies to the homeless shelters. Everyone deserved a treat every once in a while and she couldn't think of a better way to bless other people. As Tiffany sat back down to wait for the cookies to cool her doorbell rang. When she looked out of the living room window she saw two police cars. She wiped her hands on her apron and unlocked the front door to let them in.

"Officers," said Tiffany standing behind her front door as she welcomed them inside her home.

"Thank you Officer," said the detective, a dark haired Latino man in his 30's. The other officer was an older black man, maybe in his late 40's. He was well dressed and strikingly groomed.

"Thanks," the black officer said.

"What's going on?" asked Tiffany as she shut the door behind them.

"I'm Officer Benitez and this is my partner Officer Shaw. We have some information for you regarding your daughter's case. The Russian sex traffickers that you apprehended made a deal with the D.A. in exchange for information leading to the whereabouts of your daughter they were given a reduced jail sentence. They gave us the location of the white Ford Taurus your daughter was last seen in. They confessed to drowning her in the car. The car was pulled from the bottom of a lake on private property just outside of Washington D.C."

"Did they find Princess?"

"No ma'am, her body hasn't been recovered at this time; however, your daughter's blood was positively identified in the trunk of the car."

"No, no...don't say that," she broke down. The officers caught Tiffany as she almost hit the ground. They carried her over to her couch and sat her down gently.

"I'm very sorry Tiffany," Officer Shaw tried to console her.

"Somebody hurt my baby. No, no...why would anybody want to hurt her? She was just a little girl," she poured out.

"I know. I can't imagine why and on behalf of the department we extend our deepest condolences to you and your family. If there's anything we can do don't hesitate to let us know."

The backdoor swung open abruptly. Myshelle and TyRod had let themselves inside Tiffany's house when they had spotted the police cars parked outside.

"Did they find her?" Myshelle asked frantically.

Tiffany shook her head no and broke down sobbing uncontrollably.

"We're from the department, unfortunately we were informing Tiffany that the Russian traffickers were offered a deal in exchange for information on the whereabouts of Princess. A car with her blood inside was found in the lake but we haven't recovered her body yet. Our crews are doing everything they can to find her if she's out there."

"Oh my God," Myshelle whimpered.

"No, not Princess," TyRod cried.

"I'm very sorry folk. We've extended any help we can to Tiffany."

Myshelle and TyRod both wrapped their arms around Tiffany and held her as she cried and screamed out in agony. She was in the most physical and emotional pain she had ever experienced in her life. Her baby was gone.

"How could anybody hurt her? Why?"

"I know. It's not right. I'm so sorry Tiffany," cried Myshelle into Tiffany's hair.

"I just want her back. God please give me my baby back. Please, please please," she begged in tears.

"I know it hurts baby. I know. I'm so sorry."

TyRod was overwhelmed with emotions, he had to let go of the embrace and get some air. He always looked at Princess like she was more than a God daughter, she was just his other daughter. Rod had been the most influential male figure in Princess life next to Will. He felt like he lost his own daughter. He just stood on the porch sobbing into his shirt as he listened to Tiffany wail from inside the house. It sounded like someone had committed a murder all over again. It took hours to get Tiffany to calm down. She eventually cried herself to sleep while Myshelle cradled her in her arms. Rod took over running both houses so Myshelle could focus on helping Tiffany. The nightly news reported the update on the case and instantly Tiffany's phones began ringing off the hook. All of the family and friends that she didn't keep in regular contact with had seen or heard the devastating news and was reaching out to offer their condolences. Rod unplugged the house phones from the jack. Myshelle turned Tiffany's cell phone on silent.

Later that evening there was a knock on the door. When Rod looked out the window he immediately opened the door and let Will and Cindy inside. They all shared embraces and exchanges before Rod pointed Will upstairs. Will looked at his wife and gestured that he was going upstairs alone. She nodded in agreement.

"Cindy, can I get you something?" Rod asked trying to be hospitable through the pain and grief.

"No thank you but thanks for offering."

Will climbed the stairs to second floor slowly. When he got to the top he saw Myshelle sitting outside one of the bedrooms crying into the palms of her hands.

"Can I go in?" Will asked Myshelle touching her gently on the shoulder.

"I'm so sorry Will, I didn't even hear you come up here," she said getting up off the floor.

"It's okay...let me help you," he said helping her steady herself.

"She's awake now; she's just not doing that well. Go ahead inside," Myshelle opened the bedroom door for him.

"Thanks," he replied.

Will walked into Tiffany's bedroom for the first time. He had never been this far in the house, surely he had been to his daughter's bedroom but this was certainly a first and not one that he was looking forward to. When he walked in it was very dark inside, there was a sconce dimly lit on the other side of the room closest to the what he presumed to be her bathroom. Tiffany was laying in the bed covered with a blanket.

"Tiffany, it's me. I hope you didn't mind me coming up," he said sitting next to her on the bed. Tiffany never moved though her eyes were wide awake. He rubbed her shoulder gently but she still didn't respond. He waited for a few minutes hoping she would say something but she didn't.

"I'm sorry Tiffany. I feel like this is all my fault. I can't believe she might be...gone," he cried, "what type of evil person would harm our little girl. I'm just sorry. I should have protected her."

Still there was no movement or response from Tiffany. Clearly she was in a state of shock. She could hear everything people were saying to her; she just didn't have the strength or desire to communicate. So she laid there immobile and unresponsive. Her heart may have still been physically beating but sadly it was surely broken. Will tried to find words but it was evident that it didn't matter. He just sat there holding her hand in his for an hour, praying for their daughter and their families. When Will was too distraught with emotion he had to leave. He said his goodbye's quickly and gathered Cindy to leave. He promised to be back the next day.

Myshelle and TyRod stayed at Tiffany's house that night. It was no way they were going to leave her alone. Some of Tiffany's extended family wanted to come by but Myshelle knew best, so she requested that they wait to visit later in the week. Some took offense that her family would be denied access to her but Myshelle wasn't bothered or unmoved. She knew exactly who had been around and who hadn't and for the most part Tiffany had been on her own for quite some time. Her family didn't exactly support her decision to become an officer so she created a family with the people who treated her like family and loved her namely the Covington's and it just so happened that they were highly protective over Tiffany in her current state. They didn't want anyone to upset her any further than what she already was. It was a long night, the longest night of all their lives as Myshelle and TyRod waited for the sun to rise. Tiffany had nightmares off and on throughout the night and would wake up screaming covered in sweat like she had been in the fight of her life.

When Tiffany opened her eyes that morning she wanted to close them and drift back off to sleep, maybe even permanently. Life had loss it's meaning for her. What would she do with her life now? Every time she closed her eyes she saw bright blood shot red. It didn't matter how many times she blinked, the color was still there. The red made her angry, it made her feel too many of the wrong emotions about what happened to her daughter. The color red kept popping into her head along with the word: revenge.

It took her over an hour to physically get out of her bed as she lay there wide awake contemplating her next move. She tried to put the thought of revenge out of her mind but the more she tried to dismiss it, the more she got comfortable with the idea. Someone needed to feel her pain. Someone needed to pay for what happened to her daughter. Tiffany instantly found new motivation and energy to pull herself away from her bed and the depression she had already found herself drowning in. In the hour before Tiffany woke, Myshelle and Rod had managed to doze off together in the den on the couch. Tiffany didn't even bother to wake them when she got up and saw them asleep on the couch. She walked straight out of her backdoor and across the walk to Myshelle's house. She opened the unlocked door and let herself in. She walked in and found Shalonda asleep on their couch in the den.

Tiffany stood over Shalonda contemplating the best way to wake her up, she couldn't think of anything so she pulled her pistol from her waistband and drew the firearm down on the sleeping teen. The girl must could sense that her life was in danger because she woke up groggily shocked by the barrel that was pointed directly at her nose.

"Tiffany...what's wrong? Why do you have that gun pointed at me? What did I do?" she cried out.

"I have a feeling you've been lying to me and I decided that yesterday was the last day that people could lie to me or play with me. I've got nothing to lose anymore. What part did you play with my daughter disappearing?"

"I already told you everything I know. I wouldn't lie to you...with everything you've done for me," she stammered as she pleaded with Tiffany.

"I don't believe you."

"Please you've got to believe me. I told you everything."

"You're lying," said Tiffany putting her finger over the trigger.

"You would kill me after everything we've been though?"

"My daughter is dead. What do I care if you live or die? On the other hand, if you care if you live I would be real truthful really quick about the part you played in this whole thing. Something tells me there is more to your story than what you've been sharing. I won't kill you if you confess everything. NOW!" she screamed.

"Okay, okay I'm sorry Tiffany. I'll tell you the truth but you promise to put the gun down?"

"No, I don't make promises. I don't negotiate. You can live if you tell me what I want to know and if not you can die. I'll drop your sorry ass back off at your grandpa's so fast, he'll probably have sex with your dead body before burying you in his backyard."

"Oh my God, you're serious. Shit, shit! Okay, okay...Jeff paid me a thousand dollars to befriend Princess and deliver her to his boss."

"His boss?"

"Some guy. He's a white dude. He's pretty wealthy. I don't know why though and to be honest I never asked why. It was supposed to be easy money but I gave it back. I told him I didn't want to have anything to do with him or what he was doing and he told me I could live as long as I kept my mouth closed."

"So you did have something to do with it? I should kill your slimy ass right now. All this time you've been using me, laying up under me, hiding out in my house when you could have saved her all along," Tiffany continued to scream.

Tiffany's screams had awakened Tyshelle and her brothers from their sleep. They all ran to the commotion and was shocked to find their favorite auntie and God mother standing over Shalonda with her gun pointed directly at her head.

"Aunt Tiff, what's going on? What you doing?" cried Tyshelle.

"I'm sorry y'all, I didn't mean to wake you guys up but Shalonda was just telling me how she was involved in Princess' disappearance. I know this looks bad but trust me on this, go back to your bedroom or better yet go to my house. Your parents are there. You don't need to be in here for this," she sobbed.

Myshelle and TyRod's kids knew better, they didn't even play around. As much as they wanted to vouch for Shalonda and come to her rescue, the look in Tiffany's eyes meant business. They ran straight out the house to her house next door and woke their parents up.

"I'll do whatever I can to help you, I swear," cried Shalonda.

"You could have helped me months ago but you been playing these dumb ass cat and mouse games with me. My daughter is fucking dead now and you think I care about helping you now. You let my baby die," she said ready to pull the trigger.

"I couldn't tell you, I shouldn't have told you now but he threatened to kill my baby," she cried uncontrollably.

"You don't have kids."

"I do. I have a daughter. She's six months old. Why do you think I took the job from Jeff? I was desperate. My daughter has been living with a cousin of mine who agreed to help me with her if I send her money every week. I can't miss a week, a payment or else she's going to take my daughter to CPS. I was trying to get my shit together. I swear. See," she said showing her the pictures of the newborn baby in her cell phone.

"Why didn't you tell me you had a child?"

"Because I couldn't. He told me not to tell anyone!"

"Who?"

"Jeff! It's his baby. I never wanted to get pregnant but I couldn't abort another baby Tiffany. I couldn't do it again. I prayed to God for my baby to get the chance I never got in life. Jeff told me if I did this one last thing for him he would make sure that our child would be good for life. I never meant to hurt Princess or you. I just didn't know what to do and if I didn't help him he would have found someone else too. I needed that money. I need the money that he's promised to pay me until our baby turns 18."

"Make a choice, you or Jeff!"

"Choice...what kind of choice?"

"Life. Who lives? You? Or Jeff?"

"Fuck Jeff, he put me in this position. He's not my boyfriend. I didn't want to have sex with him but he made me when I got caught stealing the last time. He fucked me every which way he could, whenever he wanted to. Please kill that son of a bitch. I don't want to be bound to him for the rest of my life. My baby can do better Tiffany. I swear I wouldn't have lied to you but I didn't know what to do. He knows where my cousin lives and he's threatened to kill them all and play it off like a home invasion if I told anyone or tried to get help."

"I believe you. Never lie to me again or I promise you, it will be the last one you tell. What you told me today is just between you and I? Understand?"

"Yes ma'am, I'm so sorry Tiffany. Please forgive me. You're the only good person in my life. You and Myshelle, I wouldn't do anything to jeopardize that. I swear," she stammered.

"I forgive you. You're a child. You don't know any better. Jeff on the other hand knows better. His time is up. You, continue to stay here until we discuss your next step, okay?"

"Yes ma'am."

Tiffany put her pistol back into her waistband and left Shalonda alone in the Covington house as she went back home to get ready for her next course of action. As she exited the house, Myshelle, TyRod and their children stood anxiously on the back steps of her house as they watched her immerge from their home. She walked past them without saying a word and went back upstairs to her bedroom where she showered and dressed quickly. She stopped in her garage and pulled out a black duffel bag that she kept locked away. With her bag on her side she was ready. Myshelle stopped her as she was about to leave.

"Where are you going Tiffany?"

"To take some trash out."

"What?"

"Exactly, the less you know the better. I'll be back. Where's Rod?"

"Inside."

"I need him to drop me off downtown."

"I can take you."

"No you can't. You stay here. I don't know how this is going to play out but you stay here. If anything happens, I've been here the whole time. Tell Rod to back his truck inside of here, and I'll ride out in the backseat. I don't want to be seen leaving the house. If you're here, it's more believable. I'll be back."

"I want to go too."

"No, you can't. Rod can drop me off."

"Tiffany!" Myshelle yelled.

Tiffany ignored Myshelle's protests.

"Rod I need a ride downtown. Can you take me?"

"Of course, where you going?" he asked pulling his keys out his back pocket.

"To take care of a rodent."

"Word. Let's go," he said enthused.

"What?" yelled Myshelle in horror.

"I'm dropping Tiffany off."

"Don't encourage her Rod!"

"Myshelle when you ran up out our house to go do God knows what; did I stop you?"

"No but ..."

"I'm just dropping her off, right Tiffany?"

"Yep, I got this. Y'all have done enough."

"See, I'll be back," he said ready to go.

"Rod, back into the garage, I'll get in the backseat."

"Okay," he said picking up the garage door opener off the kitchen counter and leaving out the back door.

"Tiffany I'm worried about you. What's in the bag?"

"Stuff."

"What kind of stuff?" Myshelle asked curiously.

"The kind that kills."

"You are hell bent on revenge now huh?"

"Maybe."

"Let me go with you then. Who's going to look after you and watch your back?"

"My daughter will while I avenge her death."

"Well good God, you are serious?"

"As a heart attack Myshelle. You belong here with your family and I need you to keep your eye on Shalonda. She had more involvement than what she first told us."

"What?"

"I'll tell you later, I just don't need to be talked out of this right now. I'll be back later. If anybody comes by, I'm sleep. Okay?"

"Okay. Be careful Tiff, I love you," said Myshelle hugging her best friend like it would be the last time.

"I love you too sis. Thanks for everything. I'm planning to make it back but if for some reason I don't, I appreciate everything you've done for us," she said as the tears ran down her face.

"Don't talk like that! You've got to come back. If you get killed on me I'm going to haunt your ass in the afterlife for leaving me here. I need my best friend; you hear me?"

"I hear you. I'll see you later," said Tiffany as TyRod honked the horn from inside the garage. Tiffany climbed into the back of his big truck and laid down on the seat so she couldn't be seen. She instructed him where to take her and prayed to God for forgiveness for what she was about to do.

CHAPTER XII:

REVENGE, SERVED BEST HOT

Rod dropped Tiffany off blocks away from Jeff's apartment downtown. He stayed in one of the nice, newer apartments on Main Street that was typically a high traffic area. Wearing a dark hat and sunglasses Tiffany walked the distance to Jeff's apartment in deep thought about what she knew she had to do. Her voice of reason tried to take over but Tiffany wasn't having it. She was clearly on the thin line between sanity and insanity. She had no problems crossing that line and then some at this point. At the front door of his building Tiffany saw an opportunity to get past the locked entrance. A young mother was coming out of the door clumsily with a bulky stroller and newborn baby in tow.

"Aww, let me help you," Tiffany offered as she held the door opened and grabbed the front of the stroller to help the young women take it down the steps.

"Thanks that was so nice," the young lady said as she pushed her baby away in delight.

"Thank you," Tiffany murmured as she darted inside the door and went straight to the back of the building where the stairs were. She climbed the steep stairway 4 floors. She exited the stairwell breathing heavy but not tired. She sprinted down the hall quietly and knocked on Jeff's apartment door 417

quickly. She put her finger over the peep hole and when he opened the door

slightly she pushed the door in with all her force knocking him into the wall. She

pulled out her Taser and gave him the shock of his life before shutting and

locking the door behind her. She dragged his limp body to his living room where

she bound his hands and feet together tightly with rope she had in her duffel

bag.

She then decided to search his apartment for any clues that could help

her in the case. She tore into the drawers, closets, cabinets and everywhere she

thought there could be something hidden out of sight. She pulled pictures off

the walls and threw them into a pile on the floor. When she didn't find anything

in the main rooms she ventured back to the bedroom. She flipped the mattress

and box spring over. There was nothing hidden underneath it. Fed up she went

back into the living room where Jeff lay on the floor trying to come to but still

not knowing what hit him or who for that matter. She stood over him as he

struggled with the ropes around his hands and feet.

"Well well well you finally decided to join the party," Tiffany smiled.

"Tiffany, what the fuck is going on? How did I get tied up?" Jeff asked

nervously.

"That's what I want to know Jeff. What the fuck is going on?"

"You're going to die, that's what's going on," she said sitting down in a chair directly in front of him.

"For what? We go back Tiffany."

"That's what I thought but you've been playing me and everyone else for so long now."

"What makes you think that? I've always kept it one hundred with you."

"Where's my daughter? I want to bring her body home and bury her. You can help me with that right?"

"What? I don't know where Princess is, if I did I'd be the first to help you get her back," he lied.

Tiffany kicked him in his stomach as hard as she could, "that's for lying to me."

"Stop Tiffany, please get me up. You're going to regret this. I don't know what you're talking about."

"The only thing I regret is bringing you into our lives. I know you were involved. You can lie all day long; you will die on this floor to day like a coward should."

"I don't want to die, Tiffany stop playing," he began to yell. Tiffany had a fix for that problem. She pulled out her duct tape from the duffel bag and taped his mouth shut.

"Since your hell bent on being a liar until the very end, take that with you to your grave. I know the real you and the things you do with underage girls. I know you had something to do with Princess disappearance and what you say next will determine if you have a closed or open casket. Think carefully before you speak. I'll give you a few seconds to mull over it," she said glancing at her watch for a second before she ripped the tape off his mouth.

"Okay Tiffany, I did have something to do with Princess disappearing. I was paid to have her delivered. That's all I know. I don't know who wanted her."

"You expect me to believe that? Nigga please," she said reaching into her duffel bag for a container of lighter fluid. She began to spray the lighter fluid all over Jeff and his belongings.

"Tiffany I swear. The Russians they approached me about it months ago and I kept putting it off until they told me I couldn't hold them off any longer. So

I had Shalonda befriend her. I paid her to drop her off to the Russians. I didn't think they were going to kill her though, I swear. I kept trying to find out why but they wouldn't never say why her. I couldn't tell you, they would have killed me and my whole family."

"Like you threatened Shalonda and your baby?"

"That's not my baby."

"While I would love to see the results of a paternity test, it's not necessary. I don't believe you. Who hired the Russians?"

"I don't know. They never told me. I swear."

"Any last words?"

"Please don't kill me."

"Give me one reason I should let you live. My daughter is dead!"

"I can help you recover her body."

"If you could have done that you would have already. I don't believe for a second that you would help anyone other than your trifling self."

"Let me pay you. I've got money Tiffany. I know money can't bring Princess back but it can guarantee you some peace of mind."

"Are there other officers in our department involved?"

"I can't answer that."

"Good, I need to take a smoke break anyway," she said digging the pack of cigarettes and lighter out of her pocket.

"Whoa!"

"You were saying?"

"Danzo, Sheffield, Curtis and Linds, they have been working with the Russians too, I just don't know in what capacity."

"Thanks, I'll make note to stop by their houses on my way out. Now where's this money, if the price is right, I may let you live another day, maybe two days...who knows? Inspire me," she insisted.

"Now we're talking. Check in the bathroom underneath the sink. There's a box of cleaner in there. Take that box out. That should be fifty grand."

"What? That's all!"

"That's all I have here. There's more where that came from. I have a storage unit with at least another two hundred thousand maybe a little more."

"Where's this storage unit?"

"Belt boulevard. Number 213. The keys are in my nightstand in the bedroom."

"Let's see," she said going into the bathroom to find the money filled box. She found the lone box amongst the bottles of cleaner. Inside the box were several stacks of banded money.

Pleased with her findings, she dropped the money into her duffel bag before heading to the bedroom to check the nightstand for keys. Sure enough there was a key ring with about 5 keys on it. She dropped that into her duffel bag too.

"See I told you the truth, now let me go Tiffany. We can both walk out of here and I promise I won't say anything to anybody and I will help you find Princess's body."

Tiffany ripped a new piece of duct tape off the roll and taped his mouth closed again.

She then proceeded to spray lighter fluid all over the apartment. As Jeff panicked and struggled to get himself loose Tiffany walked out the front door and down the hall where she saw a fire alarm. She pulled the alarm first because she didn't want to be responsible for any other deaths, and even though she couldn't guarantee that pulling the alarm first would ensure that, it was a risk she was willing to take. There was no turning back. She had already gone too far and there was no telling what else she was going to do before it was all said and done with. As residents began pouring out their apartments as the sirens blared and the emergency lights flashed on and off, Tiffany went back inside Jeff's apartment coolly and closed the door behind her. She walked over to Jeff, picked up her duffel bag and took the cigarette out of the pack and sparked it, she took a puff of the cigarette and dropped the lighter on the floor causing the lighter fluid to spark into flames.

"I always thought you were a douche bag," Tiffany said finally before leaving out of his apartment. She wiped the doorknobs off completely before exiting the building through the stairway. She jogged away from the building and commotion as the firetrucks pulled up to the curb. Once she was several blocks away she ducked into a restaurant and changed clothes. She walked out of the restaurant wearing a casual business suit and tennis shoes. It looked like she had just got off work as she blended in with the other pedestrians on the street. She sped down the street until she saw a covered parking garage and walked inside to find her getaway car. The dimly lit parking garage was a carjacker's playground, Tiffany used her extensive knowledge of crimes to aid her in her getaway. Perusing the isles of parked luxury cars Tiffany saw an older white gentleman unlocking the door to his beautiful Lexus. She walked up swiftly behind him and put her gun to his back before he had the chance to turn around. She pulled a blindfold out of her pocket and handed it to him.

"Put it on," she ordered.

The elderly man complied, putting the blindfold over his head to cover his eyes. Once in place, she pressed the gun into his back further and inched him slowly toward the backseat of the car. She turned him around and helped him ease into the seat behind the driver's seat. He extended his hands out for help. She handcuffed them together and carefully lifted his legs and maneuvered him into the vehicle. She closed the door shut and picked up the keys he dropped on the ground. She got inside the car and put her duffel bag in the passenger seat.

"You're a woman? I'm being carjacked by a woman?" the man questioned from the backseat of the car.

"Would it make you feel better if I told you I was a very beautiful blonde white woman?"

"Maybe. Are you going to rape me?"

"What?" she blurted out in disbelief.

"I mean you don't have to take it. I'll cooperate," he offered.

"Listen grandpa get your mind out the gutter. This is going to be simple. I drive where I need to go. I park the car with you in it. I'll call the police within the hour and notify them of your whereabouts. The police will come and free you and you'll be on your way. And you'll live to tell the story. Maybe that will help you get some points with the ladies."

"This doesn't sound exciting at all."

"Maybe I should shoot your ass then. How would you like a hole in your ear? Maybe you can put an earring in it when I'm done."

"No thanks ma'am, as you were," he surrendered.

"Thanks I don't mind if I do. This is a nice car you have here sir. Do you mind my asking what you do?"

"I'm President of Testar Inc."

"You're a big wig...the big wig," she said turning the key in the ignition.

"Really, my wife doesn't think so. In fact, she told me I could do better."

"Your wife sounds like a piece of work."

"She is. You sound fun on the other hand. You reconsidering the whole rape thing? This could be the only action I see this year."

"Aw, Mr.?"

"Mr. Hollands, Briggs Hollands. You can call me Briggs or B-Rigstar."

"Sir is good for me. Any particular station you care to listen to?"

"No, not at the moment. I'm enjoying our conversation. You're really quite pleasant to be a carjacker. I would think this isn't your line of work."

"What?"

"Crimes. You sound very mannered, polite, well spoken. You have a beautiful voice. I can only imagine how gorgeous you are and to think I can't see your face."

"That's sweet of you, sir. I've been told I clean up well…but you are right, I don't normally carjack people. But different days call for different things so here we are."

"Yes and what a fine day for a carjacking don't you think? You mind cracking the window. I'd love to feel the breeze on my face."

"Your ride, of course," she said rolling the back window down to accommodate his request.

"So do you mind my asking what brings you into my parking deck today?"

"Tying up some lose ends."

"Sounds criminal."

"It was."

"Interesting. I detect a bit of sadness in your voice."

"For a blindfolded guy your senses are pretty accurate."

"Thanks, I think. Your troubles...is that why you are carjacking me?"

"Yes."

"Is it money related? I have lots of money; we can breeze by the ATM machine if you need to. I have lots of money. My wife may even pay a ransom for me. I take that back, no she would pay you to kill me."

Tiffany laughed for the first time in weeks, "That is so sweet of you but money isn't my problem. Can I trust you?"

"But of course, my fate lies in your hands," he reminded Tiffany.

"My daughter was killed recently."

"Oh, I wasn't expecting that. I'm very sorry miss..."

"Miss Tiffany."

"Ah, is that your alias? Cute, I like it."

"No, that's my name," she said pulling the car over and parking it alongside the street.

"What a beautiful name."

"Thanks. You know you're a pretty nice guy. If I was ever going to consider carjacking people for a living I would hope all of my vic's are as nice as you."

"I say we just ride off into the sunset right now. Beautiful gal, old guy. That's the stuff movies are made of, right," he teased.

"That would be a nice movie but the way my movie is going to play out, not so nice. It could turn into a horror movie if you know what I mean."

"So your daughter died and now you are carjacking me? I'm trying to make it all make sense."

Tiffany turned around in the driver seat and removed the blindfold from the old man's face. They stared at each other for a minute without saying anything.

"You're not that old. You deserve a happy life sir."

"And don't you Tiffany?"

"My life ended when my daughter died. My sole purpose is to see her killer's blood pour from their lifeless bodies as I stand over them watching them die."

"You really thought this movie thing out, huh?" he asked sarcastically.

"Yes I have."

"You lied to me Tiffany."

"About what?"

"You said that you were a blonde white woman. Your beauty is far deeper than that. You're a mother. I bet your daughter was beautiful just like you. I'm very sorry for you and her. Do you know who killed her?"

"I think I do."

"Well I wish you God speed on your journey. I won't report you to the police."

"It's okay if you do. I'm a police officer, or I should say, soon to be ex-officer."

"This is complicated."

"I know but I've enjoyed my time with you today. I like you a lot. I'm going to take your handcuffs off and leave your keys with you. Please stay here for at least 30 minutes before you leave."

"I will stay here an hour."

"Thanks sir."

"You're welcome Tiffany. What if I want to see you again? I've never been carjacked before," he smiled.

"Be careful in those parking garages sir."

"Here take my card," he said pulling a business card from his jacket lapel and handing it to her.

"What for?"

"My dear there comes a time in life when we all need help. If I can be of any assistance to you in your quest for justice, please call me. I would be so honored to do so."

"That's sweet sir. I can't take your card."

"Please, I'm begging you. This carjacking never happened. I'll never utter a word to anyone about this. This can be our little secret. Be safe out there," he handed her the card.

Tiffany took the card and was out of the car and jogging down the street in seconds. It's funny the people God put in our paths. Tiffany never counted on making a friend or ally when she set out to right the wrongs in her small world but Lord knows she could use all the help she could get. She hadn't figured out if she was in over her head quite yet. She didn't even know if she would live through the series of events she had laid out in her mind. She did know that somebody was going to pay for hurting the only child God had blessed her with sooner than later. Tiffany hadn't quiet figured out how she would get to the Russians confined in prison but she had crossed one person off her shit list, surely she would devise a plan to kill the Russians too. It was all a matter of time.

For today she felt good about ridding her department and city of a vial piece of excrement that posed as a public servant when he was truly wreaking havoc on the community and people he served. As she walked to the McDonald's that was adjacent to her neighborhood she finally felt alive. Taking life gave her life. It gave her power that she never felt like she had in her life. Not as a mother, police officer or otherwise. She couldn't fathom taking a life while on the job even if it was warranted by the level of threat or force. This dark side of hers wasn't a bad place to be. By now Jeff was a pile of smoldering ashes who would never have the pleasure of hurting or abusing another woman or child further. No, she didn't feel bad at all. Tiffany felt partially vindicated. Maybe the victory would be complete when she had two Russian heads in her possession. She didn't know if she currently had the strength needed to cut a man's head from his body. Weeks of grieving and mourning had made Tiffany weak and imbalanced.

Whatever her next step was, it would need to be good. She decided to take the next two weeks to train and solidify her next course of action. Soon the Russians would be dead and then what would she do. She knew her time at the police department was winding to a close. Jeff wasn't the only crooked cop out there. Every day a new video was going viral of a new case of police brutality. Every day more lethal tactics and force were being used against unarmed citizens. Maybe she would serve them up a side of her homemade justice. The possibilities were endless. Tiffany knew what she had to do and she wasn't afraid to do it.

Tiffany was the worst kind of problem anyone could ever want: an infuriated mother hell bent on justice for her daughter. No she would not wait for a judge to sentence the Russian criminals. She would not wait for God to deal with them. Taking them out was going to be bittersweet. First them, then who?

www.ingramcontent.com/pod-product-compliance
Lightning Source LLC
Chambersburg PA
CBHW030350020726
47493CB00003B/755